HIGH PRAISE FOR
DENNIS ETCHISON

"America's premier writer of horror stories."
—*Fantasy Newsletter*

"DENNIS ETCHISON IS ABSOLUTELY ONE OF HORROR'S MOST EXCITING, MOST RADICAL AND INNOVATIVE TALENTS."
—Peter Straub

"ETCHISON IS THAT RAREST OF GENRE WRITERS: an original visionary. His nightmares and fears are intensely personal, and his genius is to make us realize that we share them."
—Karl Edward Wagner

"One of the most innovative short story writers of the contemporary period . . . the most original living horror writer in America. In both subject matter and style, he has forged a contemporary horror milieu as new and daring as the film nightmares of David Cronenberg."
—*The Viking Encyclopedia of Horror and the Supernatural*

Please turn the page for more extraordinary acclaim. . . .

Also by Dennis Etchison

CALIFORNIA GOTHIC
SHADOWMAN
METAHORROR

DOUBLE EDGE

DENNIS ETCHISON

A DELL BOOK

Published by
Dell Publishing
a division of
Bantam Doubleday Dell Publishing Group, Inc.
1540 Broadway
New York, New York 10036

The introductory quotation is from *The Lizzie Borden Sourcebook*, compiled and edited by David Kent in collaboration with Robert A. Flynn (Boston: Branden Publishing Company, 1992.), copyright © 1992 by Branden Publishing Company.

ISBN: 0-440-21868-3

Printed in the United States of America

Published simultaneously in Canada

January 1997

10 9 8 7 6 5 4 3 2 1

To
STEPHEN JONES . . .
who deserves more than this for so many years
of loyal friendship.

The Borden murders are to the United States what the Jack the Ripper murders are to England. They are the two most celebrated, investigated, and unsolved mysteries in the annals of crime. . . .

There is one pivotal difference between the Ripper murders and the Borden tragedy. There is no question that Jack, whoever he was, was the murderer stalking London's East End slums. In the Borden misadventure, even after a hundred years of microscopic examination, there is no agreement among the masters of crime as to who it was who wielded the hatchet that dispatched Andrew and Abby Borden to premature graves. Popular conception is guided by the ancient doggerel that says Lizzie Borden, youngest daughter of Andrew, took an axe to them, but just as every shred of evidence indicates this to be true, those same shreds prove she did not; could not.

The Borden mystery is thus pristinely unique in the archives of mayhem, set apart from all other murders wherein the question is only whether X did it, or was it Y or X. The contradictions in the evidence have nagged aficionados since the fourth day of August in 1892. . . .

—David Kent
*The Lizzie Borden
Sourcebook*

Lizzie Borden took an axe
And gave her mother forty whacks.
When she saw what she had done . . .
She gave her father forty-one!

—A children's rhyme

Chapter 1

When the phone rang, Jenny was afraid to pick it up.

She stood in the kitchen doorway and pretended not to hear. Behind her, at the other end of the hall, the suitcases were packed and ready for the car. She racked her brain. Wasn't there something she had forgotten, an item of clothing, perhaps, even her toothbrush, that would take her to another part of the house before it rang a second time?

She turned from the kitchen and started back to the living room, but there it was again.

Ring.

"Can you get that, Jen?"

Too late. Lee had heard it, too, and now he came down the stairs, a Hi-8 video camera in one hand.

"Jen?"

"It's almost nine o'clock. Can't we just go?"

"We could." He considered, pulling at his lip. "What if it's Walter?"

"He called while you were in the shower. There's no news. He'll talk to us when we get back."

"Or my folks? I told them to check in before they leave."

"It's my mother," she said quickly, "I know it. I don't want to talk to her."

"Why not?"

"You don't know my mother."

"Don't I?"

"Not the way I do."

The phone continued to ring.

"You should have turned on the answering machine."

"I'm sorry." She had purposely left it off, hoping to get out of the house before her mother called. Jenny did not want to hear any more of her neurotic accusations, even on tape.

He started past her. "I'd better get it."

"No. Please."

He was right, of course. It could be his parents. Perhaps there was a change of plans. She had no right to prevent her husband from talking with them. Besides, she liked Jerry and Adrienne.

"I'll do it."

She returned to the kitchen and plucked the receiver from the wall on the seventh ring.

"Hello?"

"Jennifer?"

"Hi." She sighed helplessly, her stomach tensing. "Mother, we're halfway out the door. Lee says we have to leave right now or—"

"Where are you going?"

She sounded so polite, so sweet and unassuming that Jenny was almost ashamed of herself.

"I'm sorry. It's just that Lee likes to keep a schedule. We're off to Mammoth for the weekend, remember?"

"The mountains? *This* weekend?"

"Yes. I told you about it." She decided not to remind her that Lee's parents would be meeting them there, at the resort. That would be unkind.

"Oh, I'm sure you did. I forget so many things lately. . . . What about NBC? Did they decide yet?"

Not NBC, she thought. It's one of the cable networks. There was no use explaining. Her mother did not even have cable TV, she was sure. "Not yet. We're going to give them till Monday. Lee says it's better that way."

"Well, I hope so. Your own series on television . . . Think of it!"

"I have." Actually we're getting very tired of

thinking about it, thought Jenny. That's why we're going away. "It's only a miniseries."

"That's the same thing, isn't it? It's so exciting! Aren't you nervous?"

I wasn't, she thought, until you called. "There's no point, Mother. The decision's in Dave Edmond's hands now."

"David who?"

"The Head of Programming. And Walter Heim, our agent. He's taking care of everything." Then, to change the subject, she asked, "How have you been, Mother?"

"Oh, I'm fine. Except for my hip. It's the weather. But we're going to have clear skies, starting tomorrow. . . ."

Lee appeared in the kitchen doorway, looking both sympathetic and impatient. He shifted his weight awkwardly from one foot to the other in his new Adidas, eager to be gone.

"Well, Mother, don't forget that we—we want you to come visit us as soon as you can." Jenny smiled desperately over the mouthpiece at her husband. "We'd really like that. There's so much sun in California, I just know you'll love it."

"Say hi for me," said Lee.

"Lee says hi."

"Well, if you don't think I'd be in the way . . ."

Her mother's tone was still polite and unassuming, but Jenny felt her jaw muscles tightening. She's playing passive-aggressive this time, she thought, and decided to end the conversation. If it went on any longer the tightness would spread, and she didn't want to start the weekend with one of her headaches. It wouldn't be fair to Lee.

"Mother, I've got to go. Lee's giving me the evil eye." She forced a laugh, trying to make a joke of it. "But we'll call as soon as we get back."

"Have a nice time, dear . . ."

She knew Lee was waiting to hear her finish with something nice, something like *I love you*. No, she couldn't make herself say that.

"We will, Mother. 'Bye."

As she hung up the phone, she felt a throbbing in her sinuses. She squeezed her eyes shut, and missed the cradle by a couple of inches. She finally found the wall, but noticed that she had yet to hear a *click* from the other end. Was her mother listening, waiting to catch an unguarded comment before the connection was broken?

Lee took the receiver and replaced it for her. Then she felt his hands on her shoulders, turning her around to face him.

"What's the matter?" he said gently.

"Nothing. I'll be ready in a minute."

"Are you sure?" He was holding her at arm's length. "You don't look so good."

She opened her eyes and saw him standing before her, and the bright morning outside the kitchen window. In the distance, the windows of another town house flashed a blinding reflection of the sun. She moved her face so that she was in Lee's shadow and looked up at him, but his features were obscured by the backlight.

"It's just that . . ." She sought a way to put it into words, or at least a part of it, the part that would sound sane, for her sake as well as his. "She makes me feel so guilty."

"About what?"

"I'm not sure. Maybe it's because we've been married for a year, and we still haven't let her come visit."

He smiled easily. "She can come anytime she wants to, you know that. But it's two thousand miles. And I thought you wanted the room fixed up for her first. I'll send a ticket whenever you say."

"I know. It's not your fault. But I feel responsible."

"For what?"

"For her happiness, I guess. She is alone back there."

"You call her all the time, don't you?"

"She calls me. She doesn't have anyone else."

"Jen." He pulled her into his big arms and held her. "Don't do this to yourself. I'm sure she understands."

She buried her face in his sweater for a moment. But all she could see was darkness. She pushed away. "I'm telling you, you don't know her."

"I met her in Davenport, on our way back from the wedding. Remember?"

"Because she couldn't come."

"That's right, she couldn't, because she fell and

broke her hip. Do you think she blames you for that?"

"I don't know."

"Yes, you do. Now stop bumming yourself out. You're lucky to have a mother like that."

Am I? she thought. You don't understand. You really don't. And I don't know how to explain it to you.

"I guess you're right," she said. "Can we go now?"

When she came back downstairs, the suitcases were still by the door.

"Honey, I found the map. . . . Lee?"

Where was he?

"In here," he said from the kitchen.

Her first thought was that her mother had phoned again. Or had he taken it upon himself to call her? That made Jenny angry, and a little apprehensive.

"About two hours," he was saying into the phone. "If you get there before we do, ask for your key at the desk. Mom can lie down, and you can order lunch from room service, okay? Yes, I'm bringing a camera. . . ."

She came up next to him and rested her forehead against his shoulder. Please don't let me have another headache, she thought. Not today.

He covered the mouthpiece and grinned. "My dad's been ready since dawn. He's worried they'll be late."

"Hello, Mr. Marlow!" she said.

"Dad, we'd better get going. We want to grab some breakfast on the way. But you've got as much time as you need. Tell Mom we're having dinner at the Gateway Inn tonight. She'll like it."

She thought of Jerry and Adrienne, and smiled in spite of herself. Lee was the lucky one, to have parents like that. They were so funny, so full of enthusiasm. And Lee's father was a tease. She remembered that wink of his.

"Take it easy, Dad," her husband continued. "You won't need the chains, I promise. And tell Mom no one's going to break in. You'll only be gone for two days! Try to remember, this is a vacation. . . . We'll see you there."

He telescoped the antenna back into the phone and hung it on the wall, shaking his head.

"My dad," he said affectionately. "He wanted to rotate the tires, can you believe that? If I had his energy, our show would be on the air already."

She kissed him lightly on the cheek. She was feeling better. The sky outside the kitchen window was a robin's egg blue, and the mountains beckoned with clear whitecaps of snow. She could hardly wait to be on her way.

"Ready?" she said.

"Sure. I'll carry the stuff, and you lock up."

But as soon as he left the kitchen, she got the bad feeling again. She pictured her mother seated on her overstuffed couch, wondering why she had to stay at home while her daughter and son-in-law were on their way to the mountains for a vacation. Without her.

Through the open front door, she heard Lee moving the luggage down from the porch. Beyond the security wall, Saturday morning traffic zipped past the intersection and away from the city. Somewhere a dog barked, a high, nervous yipping that sounded like a cry for help.

She picked up the phone and, without thinking, dialed her mother's number.

I just wanted to tell you . . .

What?

I—I . . .

The phone rang and rang, purring softly, but her mother did not answer.

Maybe she fell again, thought Jenny, and can't get up. Maybe . . .

No. That was crazy.

She tried to put it out of her mind, and went to join Lee.

Leaving L.A., her mood improved with each mile. She watched gleaming cars shuttle back and forth between the lanes of the freeway, jockeying for position, and allowed herself to lean deeper into the headrest, cushioned and protected.

Lee rolled down the window and propped up his elbow. "Did you give Walter our number at the hotel?"

"I'm not sure. Why?"

"You're not sure, or you didn't?"

She had an impulse to tell him yes, but this

was no time to start lying. "Let me think. I really
don't know. No, I—I guess I didn't."

"Good."

"I'm sorry. If you want to stop, I'll call his service and—"

"That's fine, I said."

What did he mean? "No, it's not. I screwed up."
She sighed. "Maybe we shouldn't go out of town,
with everything still up in the air."

"That's exactly why we *should* go. I want the
network to sweat a little. It shows them we're not
worried."

"I see." In fact all she saw was Lee craning his
neck as he accelerated around a U-Haul trailer
and into a faster lane. "You're *not* worried, are
you?"

"Why should I be?" he said. "It's a lock." He
rolled up the window and straight-armed the
wheel. "We've done our part. Now it's up to them.
The ball's in their court."

"I hope you're right. We've worked so long."

Two years, she thought. All the months before
we were married, and last year, redoing the out-
line and then draft after draft of the script—and
now it all comes down to this weekend. Walter
had delivered the final version to the Head of
Programming, and it was time for a decision. It
could go either way, she knew, though Lee
refused, had refused all along to admit the possibility that they'd have to start over again at
another network. I'm sure he's right, she thought.
I should have faith in him. In us. In the project.

"Liz," he said, "has waited a hundred years to have her story told. It's a case that cries out for justice. And it won't wait any longer."

Liz. He spoke of her as if she were a living person. Of course Lizzie had been real. But she'd died in 1927. In a sense she was a silent partner in their efforts, however. Her real story had yet to be told.

"I hope the woman's angle doesn't turn them off," she said. "I tried to soft-pedal it, but—"

"That's exactly what they want now. Besides, what other angle is there?" He downshifted long enough to work his way over one more lane, then tromped harder on the gas. "She was a symbol. The suffragettes rallied around her like Joan of Arc at the stake."

"She's not exactly a martyr. They didn't execute her."

"No, they didn't. Public pressure had a lot to do with that."

"She was never completely exonerated, either," said Jenny. "A lot of people believed she was guilty. A lot of people still do. Maybe even at the Home Show Channel."

"Well, we'll set the record straight. That's what we're here for. We'll tell the world. It was Emma who—"

"You don't have to convince me. I did the research, remember?"

"I remember." He reached over and patted her knee, then floored the accelerator and slid all the way into the fast lane, inches from the concrete safety wall.

"Lee, take it easy, will you? I thought we weren't in any hurry."

"We're not."

She could hear the pressure in his voice. It wasn't because of their weekend getaway, she realized. It was about *Liz*. Lee was a strategist, playing out the endgame he had set up so patiently. But now, without knowing it, he was giving himself away, at least to her. He was not completely confident about the negotiations, regardless of what he said.

She watched his hands close on the steering wheel, the knuckles so white that the bones appeared ready to break through the skin, and his shoulders thrown back, his head jutting forward, eyes alert to any adjustments that might have to be made in order to get them where they were going. She felt a contraction behind her eyes as her breathing became shallow.

I'll bet he calls Walter as soon as we get there, she thought. He'll try to hide it from me so I won't know he's worried. But he is, God help us. Just look at him. It's not a sure thing after all, is it?

"Do you have to go so fast?"

"Relax, will you?" he snapped, then tried to cover it with a quick laugh. "I can handle it. Okay?"

Can you? she thought, sitting straight in her

seat, staring ahead. Because if you can't, who will?

"Okay," she said.

"Jerry, would you please *not*?"

Adrienne Marlow put her hands on her hips and started down the porch steps. There were cinnamon rolls in the microwave and cups of coffee on the kitchen table. If he ignored her again, she would have to reheat everything or throw it out.

"What is it, dear?" said her husband from the curb.

"I've called you three times. Don't pretend that your hearing aid's on the fritz again!"

"Are you packed, dear?" After the phone call from Lee he had come back out to the car, and now he was on his hands and knees, peering under the front end. "Once we hit the Interstate, I'm not turning back."

"I've been ready for hours. But you're not going to drive all that way on an empty stomach. Do you hear me, Jerry?"

"I want to check the brake lines." He reached under the car, then withdrew his hand and sniffed his fingers. "There's a wetness that shouldn't—"

"Jerry!"

"All right, dear!"

He locked one knee and stood, brushing off his hands. On the way into the house, he examined his blackened palms as if trying to read a road map printed there.

Adrienne held the screen door open and ushered him into the dining room.

"Wait," she said. "Wash first."

"I'm not hungry, Addy." He sniffed his fingers again. "It's brake fluid, I tell you."

"Kitchen sink," she said. "No, the back porch. Boraxo."

"But Addy . . ."

She turned his shoulders and pointed the way. "Porch. Then sit."

The cinnamon rolls were warm enough, but not the coffee. She put the cups in the microwave and set the timer for thirty seconds. When he reemerged from the back porch, she handed him a paper towel.

At the table he continued to study his hands, then held them out to her.

"I'm serious, Addy," he said. "Smell."

She placed the rolls and coffee in front of him. "You didn't wash," she said.

"Indeed I did," he told her. "But there's a petroleum base that won't come off. Do you know what brake fluid smells like, Addy?"

"I'm sure I don't. And I don't want to, either."

He took a grudging bite of his roll. "I'd better stop off at Ed's on the way."

"It's not any kind of brake fluid," she said. "There are always spots in the driveway. Besides, Ed did a tune-up yesterday, didn't he?"

"Yes, but—"

"And you trust him, don't you?"

"Yes."

"How long has he been our mechanic?"

"Fifteen years."

"That's it, then. *Isn't it.* You're just fiddling. I've been ready for hours. Now drink your coffee, and let's be done with it!"

Once she got him out of the house and locked the door behind them, he stopped going on about it. There were many miles to cover; that was bad enough, as far as she was concerned, but the Interstate would take them only so far, and then it meant driving the mountain roads, all twists and turns and no guardrail most of the time. She shuddered at the thought. Jerry, however, seemed to relish the idea, warming to the challenge as if it were another of his great adventures. With some difficulty she reached into the backseat for her down pillow and nestled into the crook between the passenger door and the seat, listening to his voice above the hum of the car.

"When will their show be on television, do you know?"

"Hmm?" The drone of his voice was putting her to sleep. She had been up since dawn, packing and making sandwiches, and now her energy was ebbing. She hoped that his was not. "I don't know, dear," she managed to say. "Sometime in the fall, I believe."

"I always knew Lee would make it," he said. "And Jenny is such a bright, articulate young person. I want to be there when they get their Oscar, don't you, Addy?"

"Emmy."

"No, her name is Jennifer."

"I know, dear. Why don't you play some music?"

He turned to the classical station, where just now a piano concerto, it sounded to her like Mozart, was in progress. The notes lilted in counterpoint to the rhythm of the tires on the pavement, pausing for emphasis whenever the car changed course, rushing out in a cascade as they picked up speed again and then settling into a gentle cadence. Her eyes closed for a moment of rest, but just for a moment, and her lips parted and curled in amusement. She was thinking of Jerry and the way he had been all morning, so happy and excited to be spending the weekend with his only son. He seemed years younger, though in truth he was as frail as ever.

At times like this it was the difference between what he was and what he wanted to be—not retired, no, but a man of the world, a man still in his prime and able to weather any obstacles— that touched her so deeply. It was up to her to be his support and his strength when he needed it, ready to dash off on a spur-of-the-moment trip, say, and not drag him down. He must never know how tired I really am, she thought. He cannot go on with a millstone around his neck. And Lee? Sometimes she almost said, *Take it easy with your father, his flesh is not as strong as his spirit,* though Jerry would never admit it, not even to himself, and it was not for her to say. Lee would realize soon enough how old they were. Until then, it was a blessing that Jerry was included in their plans. It gave him something to keep him active.

"That's not right," she heard her husband say.

What? Did he mean the Mozart? It sounded perfectly fine to her. *It sounds perfectly fine to me, dear,* she said, or did she only think it? She could not be sure.

"Listen. That's *definitely* wrong."

Whether he was right or not she couldn't say. She did not know the score that well, though it flowed in a way that sounded as right as rain, the piano notes washing over her, rocking her to sleep . . . but she mustn't sleep. He might need her to navigate from the map book. Otherwise he would get lost. And he would be too proud to admit it or to ask for help until they were miles out of their way . . .

"How are you doing, dear?" she said.

"I'm doing just dandy. It's this car that's got a problem. Knew we should have stopped at Ed's . . ."

Just then the notes ran up and off the end of the piano keyboard, clinking and squealing in a final flourish that was not at all musical, or so it seemed to her. *Would you mind turning it down?* she wanted to say and then replayed his words. *This car.* What was wrong with the car? That had

17

to be what he meant, and where the squealing came from.

She opened her eyes as a series of bass notes vibrated around her, pummeling the underside of the car. Had they hit something in the road? She was struck in the face by a shower of flying glass and shut her eyes again immediately, but not before she saw the world tipping and herself sliding off it. Then there was a moment of silence, absolute except for the whistling of the wind through the broken windshield, blowing the sharpest bits of glass deep into the corners of her eyes so that she could not open them again. The pain was sharp and terrible, lacerating her corneas. She was falling. Was she out of the car? No, her seat belt held her in place, squeezing around her waist and breasts so that when she screamed no sound came from her mouth. Had they come so far? She had fallen asleep because they were high, high in the mountains already, they must be, or else why hadn't they hit yet? She knew that the ground would be very far away and braced herself, reaching out blindly for Jerry, dear Jerry with one hand. Then a new, more terrible sound began. Don't let him scream all the way down, she prayed, and believed that her faith would be answered, but then it was too late, for the ground was already there. We never made it to the mountains, after all, did we, honey? *Oh God help us God help HIM*

Chapter 2

The service was held in the Glory Chapel of the Olympia Funeral Home and Mausoleum. At first glance it resembled a miniature Italian opera house, with ornate gold-leaf decorations and imitation marble pillars. Actually it was a trompe l'oeil of forced perspectives and foreshortened vanishing points designed to make the room appear larger, more grand. And above it all, on the stained glass dome of the skylight, Jesus held out His arms in a gesture of supplication, inviting those present to join Him in His journey between the Stations of the Cross and eternal bliss.

Shit, thought Lee.

It was what his parents had wanted, or so their instructions stated, though he could not imagine that either of them had known exactly what they were signing when they checked the word *Chapel* on the prepaid services form.

Jenny took his hand as they walked the aisle and assumed their places in the front row. Then she moved her hand to his arm and left it there to show her support. He took a deep breath. Music played from speakers hidden in the walls, behind the bas-relief angels, probably. He nodded.

"Mozart," he said.

"Is it?"

"At least they got that part right. It was Dad's favorite piece. I used to hear it through the walls at night, while I was doing my homework."

She squeezed his arm. That irritated him, and he wondered why. He could feel her concern, but that was all. He was supposed to feel a great deal, he knew. But it had not hit him yet. None of this seemed real.

"You okay?" he asked her.

"I'm fine, Lee," she said, as though it were a peculiar question.

He glanced around. There were the Wapners, Mrs. Bradshaw, even Aunt Marcie. He hadn't seen her in twenty years. He disengaged his arm from Jenny's grasp and rose.

"Excuse me for a second," he said. "I want to talk to my aunt."

"Of course."

As he stood, he noticed how small and withdrawn his wife seemed, her hands folded nervously in her lap, her head bowed. He had the impression that she was on the verge of tears, and that irritated him even more. I should be the one who's grief-stricken, he thought. But I'm not. Why?

He turned too rapidly, and lost his bearings for a moment. It was the odd curvature of the walls, the illusion of vast spaces where in reality there were none. Behind the pillars, indirect lighting gave the appearance that there were no walls, that the frescoes were windows to an outside world of olive groves and a Mediterranean sky. Where was his aunt? He could not focus on her, as she spun past in a sea of faces.

His wife was right. He should have slept last night. Or tried to. And the night before.

"Lee . . . ?"

Jenny's was among those faces, and now she touched him, providing a temporary anchor.

"Do you want to sit down?" she asked. "I'll get you a—a glass of water."

What for? he wondered. And where would she get it? His knees brushed the chairs. He couldn't risk sitting. If he tried again he might send the entire row toppling.

"I'm okay."

He pulled away from her and saw the caskets

spinning by, then the faces, then the hideous floral arrangements, then the caskets again.

They were closed.

"Mr. Marlow?" It was Pastor Johanssen, laying hands on him. "We can begin as soon as you're ready."

"Why are they closed?"

"Sir?"

"I told you, I want an open-casket service."

"That's not possible."

"Why not? I'm not ashamed of my parents!"

"If you'll come with me to my office—"

"I'm not going anywhere until you open them."

Pastor Johanssen took him aside, behind one of the pillars. "It was my understanding that the Director had spoken with you."

"Nobody spoke with me about anything."

"Because of the accident . . ."

Jenny was squirming in her chair, a pained look on her face. The others were watching now, too, from the pews. He saw Aunt Marcie dab at her eyes with a lace handkerchief.

"Let me see my mother and father."

"Mr. Marlow, you've had that opportunity."

"No, I haven't. When I got home, I identified them from photographs. And since then—"

"Sir, please—"

Lee broke away and went to the biers at the front of the auditorium. Twin hardwood coffins rested on the stands. He found the edge of the molding on one and forced the seal with numb fingertips. The upper section swung open.

Inside, he saw only satin lining.

"What is going on here?"

The Pastor was joined by the Director, a flushed, balding man with a fringe of ludicrously dyed hair. He clasped Lee on the back and spoke into his ear.

"It's too late."

"Get away from me!"

Lee went to the second casket and got the top open.

"They've already been cremated," the Director told him.

"Then why are these coffins here?"

"Mr. and Mrs. Marlow arranged for a full service. We are honoring their last request."

"Who in God's name told you to cremate them *before* the funeral?"

"Why, your wife, sir. She called yesterday morning with your instructions. I spoke to her myself."

On the way home, he glared at the road.

"Would you like me to drive?" she asked.

"Why would I want you to do that?"

"Well, that was a red light back there."

"Screw the red light."

"It was the third one in the last mile."

"Let it go, Jen."

"But—"

"I said, *Let it go!*"

"What are you so angry about? I wasn't criticizing you. I just . . . Listen, Lee. I told you I did *not* call the funeral home and tell them *anything*. I swear it! They're lying to cover their mistake. An awful, awful mistake . . ."

"All right," he said, "I believe you. And they wanted cremation. But this way, the caskets can be reused. It's grotesque."

"Yes, it is," she said. "We'll file a complaint with the Better Business Bureau."

"Why? It's too late. I wanted to see them one more time. And now I'll never have the chance. Because someone called. Or so they say."

"I don't believe it. Who would do a thing like that?"

"That's just it. If you didn't, no one else would."

"Can we sue?"

"We could." But what's the point? he thought. It's too late to change anything. They're gone.

He turned the last corner and saw a florist's truck parked in front of the condo entrance. A man in a one-piece uniform was unloading something unwieldy from the back. Aunt Marcie, he thought. Bless her.

He pulled over to the curb.

"Get out."

"What?"

"Take care of it for me, will you, Jen? I'll be home later. I have to—see about some things."

"You need to rest."

"I'm okay."

"Where are you going?"

"Just do this for me." He attempted to pull her across the seat so that he could kiss her on the cheek. She was stiff and unyielding, eyes wide, uncomprehending. "I'll be back. Trust me."

She continued to protest, but he got her out of the car and made a quick U-turn. In the rearview mirror he caught a glimpse of her standing there under the jacaranda trees, an expression of shocked abandonment constricting her features.

I have to do this.

He started back toward the civic center and the police station. After a few blocks he realized that the local cops would not be able to tell him anything. The Highway Patrol, who had discovered the accident, would have all the paperwork.

CHP Headquarters was miles away, off the 101 freeway.

The file consisted of several forms signed by the first officers on the scene, and a packet of Polaroid photographs. He held them close to his face, studying the patternless blob of twisted metal, the crushed roof of the station wagon, the broken steering wheel, the sprung doors, the collapsed bumpers, the accordion hood sprinkled with chunks of safety glass white as hailstones, as if they had made it to the mountains and the snow, after all. But of course they had not. His parents had gone off a connecting ramp only a short distance from their home in Pasadena. They had not even left L.A. County.

"What about the car?" he asked, when he could no longer bear to look at the pictures.

"Totaled," a young officer told him.

"I can see that. What I'm asking you is, what did you find?"

The officer cocked his head curiously, as if Lee had asked a very strange question. He took back the file and scanned it until he found something like an answer.

"It says here that you received the personal effects."

It was no answer at all. Lee thought of the plastic bag he had signed for at the hospital. It held the contents of his father's pockets, the wallet, a pen, some folded bits of paper, and his mother's purse. He had not wanted the blood-soaked clothing.

"Yes," he said. "That's not what I mean."

"If you want anything from the car, you have to go to CalWay Wrecking. That's where it was towed."

"Did you examine it? Not you, but the officers who were there?"

"It's all in the report. If you'd like a copy . . ."

"It doesn't say anything about the condition of the car."

The officer tried to anticipate his meaning, but got it wrong. "Don't worry, sir. A separate report goes to the insurance company. Did they have comprehensive?"

"I don't know what kind of insurance they had, and I don't care." He took a ragged breath and started again. "I'm trying to find out what *caused* the accident."

"Let's see. No indication of alcohol . . ."

"Of course there wasn't!"

"Were they on medication?"

"Not to my knowledge."

The officer flipped to the last page. "The only thing else we have is the eyewitness statement. A truck driver."

"What did he say?"

The officer perused the page, while other uniformed men and women sauntered past behind the counter, depositing other folders on desks, entering and exiting the offices beyond a maze of partitions with somnambulistic precision.

"It says here that traffic was light. The vehicle was proceeding in the far right lane, at approximately fifty-five miles per hour . . ."

"No one hit them?"

"Sir, that's correct. The vehicle veered sharply on the overpass, went out of control and broke through the rail."

"Then something was wrong with the car."

The officer looked up. He had the face of a well-trained guard dog recently off the leash, eager to please but carefully disciplined.

"More likely a heart attack. Or stroke."

"My father was in excellent health." It was too late for an autopsy. All that was left were two urns of ashes. "Something happened. They didn't just crash for no reason."

"Then it could have been mechanical failure."

"Yes, it could have been. But you didn't check for that, did you?"

Two more officers entered through the glass

doors, laughing and jangling with weaponry. Lee caught the scent of oiled leather as they passed through the lobby, on their way to a Coke machine.

"Sir, this is all I have." Already the young officer was closing the file. Other citizens were behind Lee, seated on an uncomfortable wooden bench, waiting for their turn.

He doesn't care, thought Lee. Why should he? They weren't his parents.

So I'll check it out myself.

"Where's CalWay Wrecking?"

"Over on San Fernando. But you'll have to show them authorization. . . ."

"How do I get that?"

The officer produced a Xeroxed sheet of paper from a stack behind the counter.

"Fill this out, and take a seat."

Chapter 3

The wreath was black.

It was propped up on the porch of the building when Jenny got there. Her first reaction was that it was a mistake. She turned back to the street, but the florist's truck was already driving away, only a few lengths behind Lee's car.

She read the embossed lettering across the top:

REST IN PEACE

There was no card, just a prepaid delivery receipt with Lee's name and address.

It was a joke, surely, and one in dreadful taste. The wreath had been sprayed black so that only a bit of the once-red roses showed through, dark and dead. The satin ribbon, an elephantine bow tie, was also black. Even the easel to which the wreath was attached had been sprayed, a few drops of the paint collecting thickly at the base. It reminded Jenny of congealed blood that was not yet dry.

She did not know whether to laugh or cry.

Then she felt a flush of anxiety for Lee. What would he say when he saw it? Would he think this was her fault, too? Any more of his accusations right now and she might have to go away, simply leave him a note and stay at Libby's until he had a chance to heal.

But wouldn't that only make things worse? In his mind it would be tantamount to abandoning him, running out as soon as the going got tough. And he needed her now more than ever, she reminded herself.

She stood before the flimsy easel like an artist dissatisfied with her work. But it's not my work, she told herself. I had nothing to do with this, just as I had nothing to do with the phone call to the mortuary. Did Lee believe her? Or would the suspicions chip away at their relationship until he left, too, like Rob? Though it had been eight years since her first marriage broke up, she

30

couldn't go through that again. She would rather take poison and end it now.

I'll throw it out, she thought, before he gets back. That way he'll never know.

The legs of the frame folded together, the wooden tips scraping the cement like crutches. She put her arm through it and started down from the porch, supporting the weight awkwardly on her shoulder.

"No, no!"

It was the gardener. She hadn't seen him there by the hedge. He came to her aid, his eyes twinkling.

"I do for you . . ."

"You don't have to, Paulino. It's not far." But it was all the way around the fenced-in grounds to the rear of the last building. The complex was a community unto itself, with hundreds of occupants spread over several acres. She hadn't thought of the distance involved.

He insisted on carrying it for her, much to her relief. "Where?"

"Around back. To the Dumpster."

His curly eyebrows rose in surprise.

"I don't want it," she explained.

"No?"

"No. It's a mistake."

"Very nice," he said, "this wood." He led her up again to the main entrance.

"It is?"

"Good for many things." He fumbled for the key ring at his belt.

"Here." She took out her keys and unlocked the security gate. "Why are we going this way?"

"Shortcut." He winked. "I show you."

He took her inside the grounds to a narrow path that she had not noticed before, next to the rec room, where the grass was freshly watered. The toes of her new shoes became soaked at once, with wet dirt clinging to them. There were still several buildings to pass, even using this route, until they would come to the refuse bins behind the complex.

"Do you really want it?" she said. "For the wood, I mean? If you do, you can have it."

"No!"

"Yes. It's all right, really. Just take it away. Now."

"Thank you, Mrs. Marlow!"

He started off over the wet grass to a land-scaped knoll.

"Paulino?" she said, reconsidering. "Wait."

Maybe there was a point, after all. Perhaps it had meaning to Lee and his family, as difficult as that might be to imagine, something she knew nothing about. She didn't even know who the wreath was from. Had she the right to interfere?

It's none of my business, she thought. Let Lee handle it.

"I've changed my mind," she told the gardener. "I think I'd better take it upstairs, after all. But you can have it afterwards. When we're finished. Okay?"

* * *

The wreath leaned at an angle before the fireplace, a huge black eyesore in the living room.

When he came home she would play dumb. I don't know. It was outside when I got here. Should I throw it out?

No, not even that much. Leave it to him. . . .

As the hours crept by, her nervousness fed on itself, until by six o'clock she was reduced to sitting on the couch, waiting like a faithful pet. Her stomach hurt. She rearranged the throw pillows and raised her feet, tucking her knees and holding her abdomen. She had not eaten all day; it was too late now. Her sinuses began to ache, throbbing behind her eyes. She wanted to curl up and go to sleep, just block out everything until Lee got here. But she knew that all she would see was more blackness.

In the kitchen, the phone rang.

It was a hard, brittle sound, echoing off the tiles.

Go away, she thought.

But what if it's Lee?

She got up and padded barefoot down the short hall.

"Hello?"

"Jenny? How are you holding up?"

"I'm fine, Libby," she said, relieved. "It's Lee I'm worried about . . ."

She told her friend everything: the trouble at the funeral home, the false accusation that she had authorized the cremation, Lee's mysterious departure, and now the wreath.

"He didn't say when he'd be back?"

"No. Libby, I don't know what to think. . . ."

"He can take care of himself. He needs to go off on his own, have a few drinks—"

"Lee doesn't drink."

"Or just to be alone. That's how men are. They don't know how to ask for help. And if you try to give it to them when they don't ask, they'll throw it back in your face. He's like a hurt animal. He has to lick his wounds till he feels better. There's nothing you can do. When he walks in, stay out of his way. He'll let you know if he has a thorn in his paw."

"I hope you're right." Or rather I don't, she thought. I hope it's not that bad for him. "But Lee and I always talk things out. At least we did. Until the last few days."

"I have an idea," Libby said. "Why don't I pick you up, and we can go somewhere. About seven?"

"I can't. Lee wouldn't like it."

"Wouldn't he?"

"I don't want to risk it. He needs me to be here for him, tonight more than ever."

The sound of suppressed laughter tickled her ear. "Suit yourself. If you change your mind . . ."

"I know. Thanks."

"Just don't smother him."

"I'll try not to."

This time she did not hang up but took the receiver with her to the living room. That was, after all, why they had bought a cordless phone, and it was fully charged now. Who will recharge me? she thought, and immediately felt guilty for worrying about herself. This was Lee's crisis. It was her job to be strong.

Outside, rush-hour traffic clogged the air a half-mile away with honking horns and the squealing of brakes. The dog that barked almost continuously on the next block was silent now, gone inside for dinner and human companionship. The sky over the complex turned mauve with streaks of pink; the tops of the Chinese elms and newly trimmed hedges were darkening to a solid charcoal black, the color of the shadows in dreams. In the bright window opposite her balcony, a woman puréed something in a Cuisinart, then poured it out into bowls decorated with ceramic fruits and vegetables, as Jenny's own living room grew dimmer.

Lee, where are you?

The phone rang again, an insistent chirping on the glass-topped table.

She snatched up the receiver.

"Yes?" she said hoarsely. She cleared her throat.

"Lee?" It was a man's voice.

"No, he's not here right now." Then she recognized the voice. It was their agent. "Walter, is that you?"

"Jenny, I'm really sorry about what happened. . . ."

"So are we. Just a minute."

Someone was approaching the landing outside the front door. She could hear heavy footsteps vibrating the stairs, sending an almost sub-audible throbbing through the floor. Then there was a scratching at the lock.

A key?

"Walter, I think that's Lee . . ."

The door thumped and shuddered open.

A man stood there, silhouetted against the moving branches that were etched on the sky. She tried to keep track of the seconds as her heart beat faster. For some reason she did not want to leave the protection of the couch.

"Honey?" she said, digging her fingers into a pillow.

At last he shut the door and moved into the living room.

"Why are you sitting in the dark?" Lee said.

"I—I didn't notice. What time is it?"

He made no move to turn on the light. Instead he crossed to the window and stood by the edge of the drapes. She thought his back was to her.

"Are you all right?" she said.

He did not answer.

She got up and went to him. His shoulders were stiff and unyielding. Then she remembered the phone in her hand.

"Walter's on the line."

"What does he want?"

"He called to give you his condolences." She held the phone out to him and laid her cheek against his back and closed her eyes.

"Walter," she heard him say, his voice resonating through the bones of his body and the rough fabric of his coat, "this is a bad time. I'll talk to you in the morning."

She extended her arms around his body and held him from behind. He's not better, she thought. He's worse. It's bad. He had never put Walter off like this before. The series was the most important thing in his life. Or it had been, until now.

"Then you'll have to stall them for a few more days," he said into the phone. "You know how to do that, don't you? If they won't wait, tell them to go to hell."

The dial tone crackled and went off as he thumbed the receiver, breaking the connection.

She kissed the back of his jacket and took the phone from his hand, steering him toward the couch. "Would you like anything?" She didn't know what else to say. "I can make you—"

"No."

"I don't want anything, either," she said. "Come and sit down."

She moved the pillows and held his hand.

"Somebody killed them," he said.

His words made her go rigid. "What are you talking about?"

"There was no brake fluid in the car. I went to the wrecking yard, and took a look for myself."

His voice was halting, mechanical, as if he could hardly believe what he was saying.

"I didn't know what to expect. But I checked the basics. The tires weren't flat, so it wasn't a blowout. Then I found it."

Oh, Lee, she thought, let it go. It was an accident. A horrible accident. They were killed instantly. They didn't suffer. That's all we'll ever know, and all we should know.

"I got down under the car. The hydraulic brake lines were cut. Not broken. *Cut.*"

"Maybe the workmen did it," she said, trying to sound reasonable. She had to say something.

"What workmen?"

Now she regretted saying anything at all. "The men who towed it."

"No," he said. "The lines are rubber, Jen. They weren't damaged from the impact. Someone used a sharp blade. So the fluid would leak out slowly. Drop by drop."

Why in God's name did he suspect that someone had killed his parents? The way he described it, he had begun only wanting to know how it happened. Jerry had been a conservative driver and fanatically careful with the car. Then she understood. He was asking a larger question: *Why did they have to die?* And this was where it had led him, a way of laying it to rest. For him, it was a necessary step. It was the way his mind worked, so rational and methodical.

"Did you tell the police?" she said.

"The police." He contained a bitter laugh. "I don't think they'll be very interested."

He got up and went away from her, toward the hall.

"I'm going to wash up."

She felt cold air filling the space next to her on

the couch, where he had been. Her eyes began to sting.

"I don't know what to say to you, Lee."

"Don't say anything. It's not your problem. I'll take care of it."

"How?"

"I'm not sure."

He turned on the light in the hall, on his way to the downstairs bathroom.

She sat there thinking, It's our problem. But he doesn't see that. I've never known how to be a wife to him. Won't somebody tell me, please, before it's too late?

He did not go into the bathroom. She heard him behind her, moving deliberately across the carpet, returning to stand in back of the couch.

She opened her eyes.

There in front of her, against the fireplace, was the wreath. The metallic lettering glinted in the light from the hall.

"For Christ's sake," he said, "what is *that*?"

Chapter 4

"**I**'m glad you called back," Libby said against the wind as they left the Hollywood Freeway. The top of her convertible was down and her hair was a black flame.

"I had to get out of the house," Jenny said.

"It was like I said, wasn't it?" Libby nodded knowingly. "He wanted to be alone?"

Jenny was reluctant to tell her friend all the details. Where should she begin? With the wreath that he had not believed was a prank? He *said* he believed her, but she knew better. Or the mysterious telephone call to the mortuary, by someone who used her name—or was it simply that the Funeral Director was lying through his teeth? Was it really about his parents and nothing else? Or had Lee's obsessive thinking started earlier, before they were married?

"Yes," she said. "He didn't feel like talking. He just wanted to sleep." He won't even know I'm gone, she thought. If he wakes up, I'll tell him I went to the market. "Remind me to get some eggs on the way home."

"Sure." Libby let go of the gearshift and patted Jenny's knee, a gesture of reassurance that was remarkably similar to the way Lee often touched her. "But first, I've got some friends I want you to meet."

"What kind of friends?"

"Don't worry, you'll like them. Jan and Laurie I went to school with. Lisa and Janelle are grips at the studio. Let me see. Marla and Gail moved here from Vermont last year. They're new . . ."

Why do they all sound like couples? wondered Jenny.

"And then there's Rose."

"I don't think you've ever mentioned them," said Jenny.

That was the way it was here. In L.A., everything was separate and compartmentalized, like scenes in a movie, even friendship. It was possible to know someone for months, as she had known Libby, without ever being privy to any of the players in other scenes. Lives could be played out according to the schedule on a call-sheet, with no overlap.

"You're right. I haven't." Libby turned off Sunset and downshifted around corner after corner. "We have a kind of group, you might say. Every Thursday."

The side streets climbed higher, leaving the boulevard far behind. Stars twinkled through the trees that swept past the open Miata. At the end of the block, near the top of a rise, the round face of a huge yellow moon waited on the horizon, nodding. When they reached the summit, Jenny saw what looked like a pool of liquid mercury far below, smooth and without a ripple. It was the Silverlake Reservoir. Then the car tipped forward as if crossing a knife edge and started down the other side. A smaller moon swam on the surface of the artificial lake, pacing them.

"It's beautiful," she said.

"Yes, she is."

"She?"

"The Goddess. There's a reflection of Her light in each of us, you know."

"That's a little too New Age for me," said Jenny, and laughed. Another side of her friend that had been kept from her, until now.

Libby did not laugh. Not this time. It wasn't like her to be so serious. Maybe she doesn't really want me along, Jenny thought.

"You know, you don't have to do this," she said. "If it's a party, I'm really not up for it tonight."

"It's not a party."

"I don't want to spoil anything."

"You won't."

"Are you sure?"

"Promise."

"Well, just for a little while. Not too late, though."

"You got it."

Libby made several more breakneck turns, as though they were being pursued. Then she entered an alley and switched off the ignition, ratcheting the hand brake.

"Come on," she said, jumping out of the car.

At the top of some rickety wooden steps, a yellow bug light shone like yet another moon through a dense growth of vines and rambling roses. Libby took her hand and Jenny was drawn irresistibly toward the haloed bulk, as though she no longer had a will of her own. It was almost comforting not to have to make any more decisions.

From inside, the sound of voices singing and a guitar strumming. Libby started to knock, then gave the door a push. It swung open as the song ended. The round of applause was timed so perfectly that it might have been for their entrance. For Libby, Jenny thought. They don't even know me. I'm sure they don't want to, either. I don't belong here. I should be home with Lee . . .

"Well, look who's here!" someone shouted.

Jenny entered, lagging behind.

It was an old house with a high-beamed

ceiling, knotty pine walls and a polished hardwood floor. On the floor were several handmade braided rugs, and centered on one of these was a large round table fashioned from part of an enormous barrel, with the staves sealed under a heavy coating of varnish. Around this table were sprawled nine or ten people, all dressed casually in flannel plaids and jeans or T-shirts and shorts. They got up at once to greet Libby. There were hugs all around.

"This is my friend Jenny."

"Hi! I'm Marla." A stout woman with short hair and thick glasses pumped Jenny's hand.

"And I'm Gail." A small, dark-eyed woman with thin, pale lips.

"Alma . . ." A taller woman in a deconstructed jacket and stretch Levi's.

Only now did Jenny realize that all of those present were women. It had been hard to tell at first, with the candles.

As they introduced themselves, she began to relax in spite of herself. Here was the sort of openness that can happen only among women who are old friends with shared memories, women not in competition with each other on any level. She was not one of them, and yet they accepted her without reservation or pretense. That meant they thought very highly of Libby. Why, she wondered, has Libby introduced me to her inner circle? What could I possibly have to offer?

"Libby's told us all about you," said a pretty Asian woman without makeup.

"She has?"

"Sure. You're the one who wrote the documentary."

"Well, not a documentary, exactly," she said. "More of a miniseries. A docudrama, they call it."

"When do you start shooting?"

"Oh, not for a while yet. Next season, at the earliest. *If* they pick up the option."

"I'll be watching," said Alma.

"So will I," said Gail. "It's an important story."

"I hope the network thinks so," said Jenny. "It happened more than a hundred years ago. It's not exactly hot off the presses."

"Lizzie Borden's story is more timely than ever," Gail told her with surprising fervor. "She represents the way women were treated in the nineteenth century. Like indentured servants, with no lives of their own. She washed the dishes, ironed the clothes, made the meals . . ."

"Things sure have changed a lot, haven't they?" said Alma, and everyone laughed.

"They did have a maid," Jenny said.

"But did *she* have a life? Did Lizzie? A forty-year-old woman, still living at home!"

"Thirty-two," said Jenny.

"Think of it! All to serve her father!"

"Well, her mother, too. The stepmother, Abby . . ."

"It was the father, don't you see? He held all

the cards. Did the women have any money of their own?"

"Actually, Lizzie and her sister . . ."

"Any *real* money? The only hope was that he would die, and leave them what was really theirs! Lizzie was America's first feminist! When she couldn't take it anymore, when she finally acted in the only way that was possible for her, the press—the *male* press—crucified her!"

"The point of the story," Jenny explained, "is that she didn't do it. She knew who committed the murders, but she refused to say. No one else was ever charged, before or after she was acquitted. She took the secret with her to the grave."

Alma was shaking her head. "It doesn't matter who killed them. What matters is that she was put on trial for all of us."

Jenny thought, That's an interesting interpretation. It may or may not be true, but would it work? *Saint Lizzie.* No, it was too late to change the script. The last draft was done.

"I'll have to think about that," she said.

The candles began to flicker. The table was rocking. How could that be? Jenny saw no one near it. All the women were gathered around her.

"Hold that thought," Libby told her. "Right now, there's someone else you have to meet. Someone special."

It was the wooden floor *under* the table that was moving, vibrating as if in response to an aftershock from the San Andreas Fault. Then the circle parted, and all heads turned to a stairway in the corner, as a large woman in a caftan descended to the living room.

Libby and Alma went to the foot of the stairs and helped the large woman find her footing. They steered her to the table.

"This is Jenny," Libby said to the woman. "Jenny, meet Rose."

"Hi," said Jenny. She was at a loss. Finally she extended her hand. Then she saw the woman's eyes. They were milky-white. She's blind, Jenny thought, startled.

The woman's head turned, turned again, seeking the source of the voice, and zeroed in. Jenny had the uncanny feeling that the eyes were staring directly at her, as if from behind opaque contact lenses.

"How do you do, Jenny Marlow?" She was at least three hundred pounds, and tall, taller even than Lee. Her hair was cropped close, but that only served to emphasize the dimensions of the woman's skull. She had a thick, overhanging brow, which made her eyes appear small, deep-set in massive sockets. The overall effect was of a powerful, almost primitive strength. "Let's sit down now."

"Here, Rose." Libby helped the woman settle her bulk into a large rattan chair at the table. The chair creaked.

Will it hold? Jenny wondered.

Alma dropped to her knees and sat on the woman's right, folding her legs under the table.

Gail, Marla and the others took their positions on the floor.

"I have a question," Alma began.

"Not yet," Rose told her. "Does everyone have enough wine?"

"Marla?" Gail lifted a half-gallon of Napa Valley chablis.

Marla refilled her glass and passed the jug around. In the warm glow of the candles, each face was captured and reflected in the long-stemmed glass before it, with a faint distortion added.

There was an empty space at the table, Jenny realized, across from Rose. Even an empty wine-glass. She sat down on the rug as gracefully as she could.

"No, thank you," she said when Libby started to fill it.

"Sure?"

I haven't eaten anything, thought Jenny. It will go right to my head.

On the other hand, it would ease the pressure of thinking about Lee, about all that had happened in the last few days. And if she needed anything, it was to forget, to blot out of her mind, however briefly.

"Well, maybe just a taste."

Libby poured. The candles flickered as glasses were raised. Jenny could swear that Rose was looking at her. She averted her eyes self-consciously and tasted the wine.

"You look nice tonight," someone said. "Did you do something new with your hair?"

"I thank Janine for that," Rose said.

Which one was Janine? Jenny sipped more of her wine, scanning the table furtively. There were five to her left, six to her right, counting Libby. Plus herself, and Rose directly opposite.

"It was just a trim," said a young woman with long hair woven into cornrows. "Maybe a little D'Iffray holding gel."

The others laughed, setting the candles to flickering again.

"Can you get me some?" asked a woman with gold-loop earrings.

"I'll bring it next time," said Janine. "Or you can come by the salon."

"I will. Thanks."

"What about partnerships?" asked Janine.

"In what respect?" said Rose, who knew somehow that the question was directed at her.

"Well, I'm thinking about investing in the salon," said Janine. "I was wondering if this is a propitious time."

"You may ask," Rose told her.

Ask? thought Jenny. She just did ask, didn't she?

"All right," said Janine, "who are the Companions for this enterprise?"

"The Companions," said Rose, "are two, but neither is of any consequence in the present inquiry. One is a former doctor of medicine, the second a housekeeper and seamstress. Neither wishes to communicate at this time, so they need not be considered. There are no barriers to any partnership."

"I see," said Janine.

"Do you, dear?" said Rose, blinking her blind eyes for the first time. "I don't!"

The others joined in her laughter.

Jenny did not know how or when it happened, but an invisible boundary had been crossed, so that now the conversation was on a different plane. The shift was subtle but unmistakable; they had been making small talk, and then they were talking about something more elusive and abstract, using a secret vocabulary. *Companions*. What did that mean? They seemed to understand. It was a ritual or ceremony of some sort, apparently, and everyone was in on it. Everyone except Jenny.

"I have a question about travel," said Gail. "Marla and I are thinking of going to St. Croix in the fall, but she doesn't like to fly, and I get seasick on cruise ships. I'm willing to take Dramamine, but I was wondering—we were wondering—if there are any negative auguries?"

Rose responded easily, as if carrying on a side conversation, one that did not engage her full attention. Her eyes remained directed at a point somewhere near Jenny's head; it was impossible to be sure, because the pupils were not focused.

"The Companions are many and varied in this case. All were once slaves in what is now known as Antigua, prior to the arrival of Captain Mission in the seventeenth century, who liberated them under the Articles of Freedom. The Primary Companion is a Freemason who was Mission's first mate. He observes that the climate of freedom has long since departed, and the old ways have returned to the islands. Any travelers to the area might wish to note the encroachment on former liberties, and arm themselves accordingly."

"*Arm* themselves?" said Gail. "You mean with guns?"

"The real battlefield is in the mind. Armor made of light contains all colors and deflects the darkness, which is defined as the absence of color."

"Okay, then," said Marla. "Are you up for it?" she asked Gail.

The two women interlaced their fingers. "Why not? Let's go for it!"

This, thought Jenny, is a séance. It must be. She couldn't believe what was happening; Libby had never hinted at any interest in the occult, never once in all the time they had known each other. And what a strange kind of séance! There was no dimming of the lights, no billowing curtains and spirit voices and ectoplasm. The medium did not even go into a trance. It was all so ordinary, so matter-of-fact. As if it were a part of their everyday lives.

She leaned over and whispered into Libby's ear. "What are Companions?"

Libby put a finger on her own lips.

Rose's round white eyes adjusted in tiny increments until they located the whispering. Could she see, after all?

"Do you have a question, Jenny Marlow?"

How does she know my last name? Jenny thought. No one had said it. She felt pinned like a butterfly to the braided rug, unable to get away. Nobody moved. And yet the candles flickered again, as if a breeze had entered the room and was about to snuff them out. A wisp of black smoke rose from the wick in front of Jenny. Above the guttering flames, Rose's massive head loomed in the yellow glow, floating on the fire.

"Me? Not really. I'm just listening."

"You have a question." This time it was a statement. "Don't be afraid."

"I'm not." She tried to laugh, but her throat was dry. Every other face was watching her, too. They were friendly but neutral, waiting to see how she would play her part.

"Don't move away from the light. . . ." Rose began.

For the first time the woman lowered her head, releasing Jenny from the grip of her blind stare. Around the table wineglasses suspended in the air, lips parted expectantly, smiles froze. Something out of the ordinary had begun. They were watching and listening to find out what would happen next.

Rose's head tipped upright again, and now her eyes were even wider, no longer implacable but round and alert, awakened by an inner vision of such intensity that Jenny all but expected to see it projected onto the dancing light and smoke-filled air over the table.

"The Companions are two. . . ."

Her voice rose an octave, like a violin string tightening up. Jenny felt the new, higher pitch alive in the air between them, testing the strength of the thin crystal glass near her hand. In the convex surface of the glass she now saw something move: a face, long and squeezed, as of a homunculus imprisoned in a bottle, desperate to escape. Was it her own face?

"They are sisters. One serves the light . . . and one the darkness. The light is dimming, and the other comes near . . . the blade! I see the blade . . . *the blade that falls!*"

Rose slumped forward, her features slipping below the line of guttering flames. Where her head had been there was now only the pane of a tall window, and beyond that the darkness. Within the darkness, Jenny saw an image of the table, with the candles in the center and twelve faces turned to the night.

"Are you okay?"

Alma put her arm around Rose's shoulders, supporting her.

"Rose!"

Janine was at her other side, shaking her.

The table rocked unsteadily and one of the wineglasses teetered and fell over, shattering. The chablis spread in a pallid inkblot across the tabletop, darkening rapidly against the varnish.

Jenny snatched her hand away before it touched her fingers, but it dripped over the edge and onto her skirt. Candles tipped, hot wax sizzling in the wine and bubbling blisters into the table.

Rose sat up straight, shrugging off help.

"What's the matter?" she said. "Did I doze off?"

"I guess you did. . . ."

"You said . . ."

"I didn't say anything," Rose told them. "Not anything at all. Is that clear? Now . . . are we quite finished for the evening?"

Chapter 5

Around eleven P.M., he heard someone in the house.

He did not know what had awakened him, or whether it was anything at all. The last thing he remembered was stretching out on the bed for a couple of minutes, just long enough to rest his eyes. He had been listening to the whisper of distant traffic, a motorcycle passing at the end of the block, the crickets in the hedge below the bedroom window, and the tinny, canned voice of a game show host from the TV set next door. The voice was interrupted constantly by the clicking of a wheel as contestants spun for the words that would bring them fame and fortune. . . .

The next thing he knew, he was in front of his parents' home in Pasadena.

His father got down on his hands and knees and peered under the station wagon. What he was looking for Lee didn't know, but it had something to do with the tires.

"I can do that for you, Dad," he said.

His father wouldn't listen. *"That's all right, son. You have a script to finish. . . ."*

"It's finished. Anyway, I already checked the tires, and they're fine."

"Maybe it's not the tires. Something doesn't sound right."

"Let me. You'll hurt your back."

A gang of motorcyclists roared by. His father didn't hear what Lee said and got under the car, squinting at the tie rods. Lee continued to reason with him, but it was hopeless.

"Get me the jack, will you, Lee?"

"You don't need to do that. . . ."

"The jack. In the trunk."

The last of the motorcyclists passed. Lee stopped arguing. He opened the trunk and took out the jack. At the front of the car, all he could see was his father's greasy hand, waving him closer.

He set up the jack and began to pump. As the tire lifted free of the asphalt his father turned onto his back and worked his way under.

"Time for breakfast!"

It was his mother, on the porch.

"Be right there, Mom," he called. *"As soon as Dad finishes . . ."*

"What?"

"I said, Dad wants to check the . . ."

"What? I can't hear you."

She had forgotten to buy a new battery for her hearing aid. I should have done that for her, he thought. He could pick one up at the drugstore a few blocks away. It was no problem. Except that she wanted him inside for breakfast now—both of them. It would do no good to tell her that he was not hungry. She believed in three square meals, and as long as he was at their house he had no choice.

His father would have to wash up.

"Come on, Dad."

"What did you say, son?"

"Mom—"

"I'm almost finished. Tell your mother we'll be ready to go in five minutes. And if she's not packed yet, it's too late. I want to keep to the schedule, or we'll never get there!"

He looked up at his mother, who pursed her lips at him from the porch, and shrugged. She was in no mood to be put off. He'd better go inside and hope that his father followed.

As he walked around the car, his foot brushed the jack handle. He glanced down. The jack still held.

It was not until he got to the porch that he

heard the hissing. What was it? Dad was right, he thought. He must have found a slow leak in one of the tires. Ahead, in the hallway, his mother greeted him. Then her eyes widened and her mouth opened. Was she about to say something? *You've gotten too thin, Lee* or *You'd look so much better with a haircut* or *You didn't wipe your feet!* But no, she was looking past him, through the screen door.

Lee turned to look with her, as the hissing grew louder, followed by a resounding crash.

The car rocked on its springs, settling lower, pinning his father to the pavement.

That was where the hissing came from, he thought. Not the tire—the jack! The pneumatic pressure had leaked out until there was not enough left to hold the weight and the car slipped off the stand and onto his father's chest.

"No!"

He ran out of the house and down the steps, a terrible fear inside him. His father's legs were not moving and there was no further sound, not so much as a grunt. He saw a rivulet of motor oil trickling out from under the car, spreading in a pool. When he got there he saw that it was not oil. It was blood.

He hooked his fingers under the bumper and tried to lift the car. He put his back into it. But it was no use. He felt tears running from his eyes, dripping down his cheeks, coursing off his chin and onto the pavement in dark splotches, one drop at a time, as his throat convulsed and his lips moved but no sound came out. . . .

One eye popped open, his eyelashes brushing the pillow.

He was awake again.

It had not happened, of course.

But the slipcover was wet.

That part was true . . .

He raised his head an inch, two inches, trying to see across the dark bedroom. What had awakened him? The house was silent as a tomb. But something had called him back to consciousness. It was the feeling he had had as a child, suddenly wrenched awake in the night by the certain knowledge that someone, some*thing* was with him in the room, just out of sight behind the dresser or the closet door, something that would not show itself unless the time was right. And only *it* would know when that time came.

Then he heard it.

In the living room, a scratching at the door.

And a whispering sound, followed by a muffled thump, as the front door opened and shut.

A few seconds of absolute silence, broken only by the hissing of his own pulse in his ears.

Then the scratching again . . .

This time at the bedroom door.

Whoever it was had ignored the rest of the house and come straight for him. Whoever or whatever it was, *it knew*.

The bedroom door eased open, brushing the carpet.

A dark, very dark shape was standing there.

"Lee? Are you awake?"

Jenny.

Of course. What had he been thinking?

He pretended to be asleep.

He heard her shedding her clothes, then felt the bed sag as she slipped in next to him. He forced himself to breathe evenly, regularly again. He felt the palm of her hand on his back, and soon her arm sliding around his body from behind. She kissed his hair and laid her head down on his pillow.

After a few minutes he started to drift off. He did not want to see what was taking form in the granular shadows before him. He took her hand in his and drew it the rest of the way around him, clasping her fingers tightly.

"Lee," she said. She had known that he was awake; he could tell by the tone of her voice. "How are you doing, honey?"

"Okay."

"Sorry I woke you."

"You didn't. I was—having a dream. I didn't want to sleep anymore."

"What kind of dream?"

"A lousy one."

"I'm sorry."

"It's not your fault." He did not want to talk about it. "How's your friend?"

"Libby? Oh, she's fine. I should have called. But I didn't want to wake you, if you were asleep."

"That's all right." I'm glad you're here now, he thought, but could not say it.

"Did you eat?"

"I found something. Don't worry about me."

"But I do." She held a breath and let it out so slowly that it caught in her throat. "It's all been so awful . . . for you, I mean. I shouldn't have left."

"Yes, you should have. I'm no good to you right now."

"I want to help," she said. "I don't know how. Tell me what you need, and I'll do it."

"I don't know. I don't want anything."

"That's just it. I feel so useless. . . ."

"It means a lot just having you here." It was hard for him to say. But she needed to hear it. And it was true.

He turned over then, held her to him, and buried his face in her hair. He felt her body jerking as she sobbed silently. When he smoothed her hair, comforting her, he felt dampness where his face had been, and knew that he was crying, too.

After that he sank into a dreamless sleep for the rest of the night. It was the first time in several days.

He felt warm breath on his face, and opened his eyes.

The sun poured in through the open curtains.

There was no one else in the room. What he had thought was breathing was only a swirl of air, a current stirred into motion by the movements of the bedroom door.

Soon he heard Jenny in the kitchen, the hushed dripping of the coffee machine and the crunching of toast as she buttered it. And her voice. She was talking to someone. He could not make out the words, only the tone. It was impersonal, businesslike. Then her slippers on the carpet as she left the kitchen and came upstairs again.

"You're awake." She had the telephone in her hand but the red light was off; she had broken the connection.

"What time is it?" he said.

She glanced over his shoulder at the clock radio. "About nine. You had a good sleep."

"I have to get up."

"Why? I can take care of everything."

"Can you take a morning piss for me?"

"Oh."

He dropped his legs over the side of the bed and trudged into the bathroom. When he came out, she was back in the kitchen. He went down and found her staring into space over a cup of coffee. She saw him and forced the muscles of her face into a cheery smile.

"Who was that?"

"When?"

"A minute ago. You were talking on the phone."

"Oh, just Walter."

She tried to make it sound casual, but he could hear from the closed, glottal tightness in her throat that it was not casual at all.

"What did he want?"

She finally had to answer. "The Home Show Channel called."

"Dave Edmond?"

"Yes, I think so."

"You think so, or you know so?"

"Walter said not to worry. They're taking their time."

There was something more that she was not telling him. "And?"

"And nothing."

"Are you sure?"

"I'm sure." She fidgeted.

He poured himself a cup of coffee and sat. Was she telling the truth? "That's a good sign," he said.

"Is it?"

"The longer the jury is out, the better our chances."

"Good. That's good, then." She sipped her coffee.

"Was I dreaming," he said, "or did I see a black wreath in the living room last night?" He had been so tired that he could not be certain about anything.

"I wish you had been dreaming. If you were, so was I. It was on the porch when you dropped me off. I just missed the delivery man, so I don't know who sent it. There was no card."

He looked down the short hall to the living room but saw only the fireplace. "Where is it?"

"I threw it out. Honey, who would do such a thing?"

"Send us dead flowers? I'd sure as hell like to find out. Maybe it was Morton, the Funeral Director. He's not exactly overflowing with Christian charity, if you know what I mean."

"It was probably a mistake," she said.

"Some mistake! If it was, I could sue that florist's ass off."

"Or a joke. A sick one."

It all came back now. The concerns of the last few days crowded into the kitchen, illuminating the appliances with a gleaming edge, as though some reflection of movement were about to be revealed in the curved silver handle of the refrigerator, the window in the oven and the glass coffeepot. He felt reality settling over him, and the need for action.

He remembered his trip to the CHP, the wrecking yard, what he had found in the remains of the car: the thin, sharp cuts in the lines from the master cylinder.

"You should rest today," she told him. "Don't even answer the phone."

"I have to follow up on something."

"I can run things for a while."

"Can you?"

"Let me. Please?"

You can't do it for me, he thought. I'm afraid you wouldn't know how. I'm not sure *I* know how, but I've got to try. Somebody sabotaged the station wagon, which means that what happened was no accident. I wish it were, but it wasn't.

"Just some errands," he said. "I can handle it."

"Not that business about the car? Let it go, Lee. There's no way to . . ." She stopped herself.

"Bring them back?"

She did not go on.

"That's what you were going to say."

"No, it wasn't. Just take it easy. If you start turning over rocks, you're going to find dirt. Don't go looking for it."

There was no point in arguing. He knew what he knew. He finished his coffee in a scalding gulp. "I'd better take a shower."

"Okay. Then it's my turn."

He pushed away from the table. "Are you going out?"

"I'm meeting Libby for lunch later, at that place she likes. You know. Plus we don't have any food in the house. What do you want for dinner?"

"We'll get take-out," he said.

"I can whip something up. I don't mind."

He decided to drop all pretense. "Are you going to take the meeting?"

"What meeting?"

"With Dave Edmond. I know his style. If he called Walter, he's ready."

"No! I wouldn't know what to say."

"Good. It's better if we wait. Talk it over with

Walter, if you like. But tell him I want them to sweat a little longer. The more we wait to get back to them, the more they'll want it. They'll think we're talking to someone else."

"Right. I agree."

He hoped she saw it his way. But he did not want to get into it. Later, he thought. Tomorrow. Next week. When I've had time to hire a private detective to find out about the car. I have no choice. The police won't touch it. They don't have much time for mysteries.

Chapter 6

Jenny hated to lie to her husband.

Well, she told herself, it wasn't really a lie. More along the lines of a good deed, a white lie. She agreed that they should wait a few more days before taking a meeting with the cable network, but in the meantime she saw a way to bolster the project by actually *emphasizing* the woman's angle rather than downplaying it, and that was worth running by their agent.

If she was right, she would help Lee in a way he'd never admit he needed—couldn't admit, because that would mean acknowledging some inadequacy about his own plan. It wasn't that there was anything wrong with his plan; after all, they had come this far with a project that began as nothing more than a notion. . . .

God only knew where it came from. One night they had watched a rerun of an old movie-of-the-week about the accused axe murderess. Then Jenny had picked up a few books at the library. By the time she finished the first one, it was clear that Lisbeth Stewart Borden was innocent. The job of police departments was to make arrests, the job of district attorneys to produce indictments, and Fall River, Massachusetts, in 1892 was no exception to the rule. They had to arrest someone; Lizzie was the most obvious suspect and, though she was far from the only one, after her acquittal no other person was ever charged. Jenny might have suspected a cover-up to protect the privileged, as with Jack the Ripper, except that the real killer was no more connected than Lizzie, who was the daughter of a successful businessman.

So Jenny had put together a viable theory, based on the best available evidence, and before long she was convinced that it was the only possible answer under the circumstances. That in itself was interesting, the basis for a magazine article or even a book, perhaps—but it was not until Lee got involved that the project began to take shape. . . .

And now there was more.

There was a hard kernel of truth in what Libby's friends had said last night, a new angle that might strengthen their pitch. It was her ace in the hole, her chance to contribute something to the negotiations.

She couldn't wait to tell Walter.

She took the Ventura Freeway to the 405, drove south for a few miles to the 10 East, and got off at Santa Monica Boulevard.

Walter Heim's office was on the fifteenth floor of the Century City Towers.

The elevator opened directly in front of the Creative Artists International office. She wanted to slip into the ladies' room for a moment, long enough to check her hair and makeup in the mirror.

Before she could turn away the office doors opened and two men hurried out. They saw the elevator closing and hustled to catch it. One wore a shiny, expensive suit with baggy trousers and Italian loafers; the other, much younger, had on Guess jeans and an oversized Hawaiian shirt with several buttons undone. She hesitated as they brushed past her. Inside the office, in the reception area, she saw a secretary in a silk blouse, taking calls.

No point in stalling, she thought. It's now or never.

She walked forward, head down.

"Look at it this way," the man in the baggy suit was saying. "It's thirteen weeks, plus residuals."

Dennis Etchison

"I don't give a rat's ass," said the one in the colorful shirt. "It's a supporting part!"

"A *recurring guest spot*. And it will put you back in the mix."

They pushed a button in the wall and waited. Then they noticed her still there and dummied up. But Jenny was not looking back at them. She was hoping to see herself reflected in the polished elevator doors. When they closed, the image that came back to her was blurred and distorted, like a fun-house mirror. That didn't help her state of mind; it was the way she felt already. She shut the office doors behind her and faced the receptionist.

"Jenny Marlow," she announced, approaching the desk.

"Jenny . . ." the secretary began. She paused and pushed a blinking light on the phone. "CAI. Please hold." Another light. "CAI. No, he's not in. Would you care to leave a message?"

She repeated this routine several times. When there was a message she wrote it down in a log book and went on to the next call, and the next. Eventually she had an opportunity to glance up again.

"Jenny . . . ?"

"Marlow. To see Walter Heim."

"Is he expecting you?"

"Yes." It was as good as true. Walter would want to see her.

The telephone lights were blinking again. The receptionist dialed an extension. "I have a Jenny

Murrow here to see Walter." Then she switched lines. "CAI. Please hold . . ."

After a couple of minutes, a male assistant appeared and led Jenny down a long hall to Walter's office.

"Can I get you anything? We have Evian, Perrier, cranberry juice . . ."

How about a vodka rocks? thought Jenny.

"Constant Comment, Celestial Seasonings . . ."

"Coffee?"

"Regular or hi-test?"

"Just decaf. Please."

Walter had a corner office, with tinted windows on two sides. The shelves on the third wall contained a few books and a lot of plants, framed photos of children from several marriages, an autographed baseball in a Lucite stand, a Super Soaker water gun and a collection of Japanese modular toys. The fourth wall held stacks of Xeroxed scripts with titles written in black marking pen on the edges of the pages. While she waited, she scanned some of the titles: *Cruisers, Physical Attraction, Big Buddies, Love Positions, Wet Nights, Rooms in the Heart, Termination Day, Get Out of My Life, Why Don't You, Babe?, Show Me the Way to Go Home, The Insomniac, Valley of the Shadow, Now I Lay Me Down, Icepick, Pushing Up Miss Daisy . . .*

Walter entered at his usual flat-footed pace, paused long enough to touch her hand coolly and sat behind the desk.

"Jenny," he began awkwardly. " I didn't expect to see you here. How's Lee taking it?"

"The only way he can take it," she said. "Hard. He decided to lay off for a few days. There's the will, the estate . . ."

"You look like you're holding up." He rearranged papers on his desk. "Give Lee my sympathy. If there's anything I can do . . ."

"There isn't. Hello, Walter."

With the preliminaries out of the way, Walter changed gears. He tipped back in his contour chair, his head almost touching the window.

"The Home Show Channel wants a meet," he said.

"When?"

"This afternoon."

"That's not possible," she said immediately.

"Then we pass and go to Fox. As soon as Lee's ready."

"Wait a minute," she said. "Just like that?"

"They brought in a new man, and he wants to firm-up the fall schedule by the end of the week."

"But we have another month."

"Not this year. The word came down this morning. They're premiering the new lineup a month early, to beat the majors. We don't have a choice."

"Lee's not ready!"

"What about you?"

So this was it. Either they made the fall schedule, or it was back to square one at another network. Lee's plan had a flaw, after all.

"I've been ready for months, Walter, you know that. But I can't pitch it without Lee."

"It's not a pitch session. They want to meet you."

"Everything's on paper. You have the pages, and so do they. It's all worked out."

"They don't like to read. They have people who do that for them. The coverage has been favorable. Now it's time to play ball. They have a contract with Lindsay Wagner. Is there a part in it for her?"

"Well, she's six feet tall, for one thing. Lizzie was five-three."

"Lawrence of Arabia was five-six," said Walter. "Peter O'Toole is six-three."

"But this is supposed to be a docudrama."

"Correction. This is television. Do you want it or not?"

"Of course I do. We both do."

"Then we play the game. You've got one strike against you already. The project is writer-originated. They don't like writers in this town."

"Look, Walter . . ."

The door opened, and the assistant set a mug of steaming black liquid in front of Jenny. That gave her a moment to think. When the door closed, Jenny looked up at Walter without blinking.

"This isn't a game," she said.

"It's not?" Walter was bemused. Behind him, the shops and theaters of the Schubert complex were bustling with activity. From this height the

73

tiny dots pouring in and out of the buildings might have been worker ants.

"I thought you cared about this project," she said.

"I do. But it's more than a notion. You're either in or out. It can get mighty cold out there. You might as well be King Kong standing on the roof, pounding your pud. There's no way to go except up or down."

She saw the harsh, merciless nature of the perpetual sunlight outside, as if the tint on his office windows had peeled back, exposing her to its full glare. She felt their project slipping away, and imagined Liz taking a swan dive off the top of the Twin Towers, falling past Walter's window and splattering on the pavement below, and herself falling, too, and Lee. Or would *Liz* fly? There was nothing else to hold onto.

All she knew was that she could not let Lee fail. If she was not able to do even this much for him, be his strength when he needed it most, then what good would she ever be to him, or to herself? She had to give it her best effort. Nothing less.

"What do I have to do?" she asked.

The meeting was set for one o'clock.

She and Walter arrived five minutes early and waited on an L-shaped sofa in the lobby. The magazines were of no interest to her. "Di and Fergie: An Unexpected Romance," teased the cover of *People*, while *US* announced the latest news about the rehabilitated Michael Jackson and his ill-fated mechanical dinosaur. *Fifty handicapped children from City of Hope Hospital entered the behemoth's interior, and forty-nine boarded the bus at day's end. But Michael won't give up his search for little Peter, even if it means dismantling the creature bone by bone . . . !*

A young man with no sideburns and an oversized white shirt showed them in.

"Can I get you anything?" he said. "Ginseng cola, New York Seltzer, Yoo-Hoo?"

"No, thank you," said Jenny.

Walter ignored him, flicking through the papers in his ostrich-skin briefcase.

They were ushered into a bare room with framed photographs of several television stars on the walls. The only one Jenny recognized was Bill Cosby. He was smoking a very large cigar and smirking cutely, as if he had just spilled Jell-O on the lap of his Armani Black Label suit. There was a long table with yellow legal pads and ballpoint pens set out neatly by every chair. The room smelled of paint and disinfectant, as though the furniture had only been added after a thorough delousing, once the previous tenants had vacated.

A short, stout man wearing a satin Dodgers jacket and baseball cap entered first.

"Walter!" he said. "Thanks for the box seats!"

"Tip," said Walter, "I'd like you to meet Jenny Marlow. Jenny, this is Tip Topp."

"Hi! That's Pete Pollen. . . ." Three more people

entered and took seats at one end of the table. "And Kurt, and Kebrina."

They all exchanged cursory nods.

Then Jenny sat down next to Walter, at the other end.

"I looked at your proposal," said Tip.

"Have you?" said Walter off-handedly.

"Yes," said Kebrina.

"It's brilliant," said Tip. "I really like the woman's tragedy angle. Here's this girl, Birdie . . ."

"Brigitta," said Kebrina.

"Whatever," said Tip. "She comes to this country as a poor orphan immigrant, goes to work for a rich family, and then the shit hits the fan! But she's loyal to her employers, or at least her employers' daughters, and . . ."

"Excuse me," said Jenny, "but who are we talking about?"

"The housekeeper, what's her name?"

"Bridget Sullivan?" said Jenny. "She's a minor figure . . ."

"She's Irish, right?"

"Originally. I don't see . . ."

"I see Nicole Kidman, don't you?"

Kurt nodded vigorously. "Who else?"

"Can we get her?" said Tip.

Pete shrugged. "Where's she going in features? Doo-doo time!"

"But it's not about Bridget," said Jenny. "It's about Lizzie."

Tip looked at her blankly. "What's the point? Everybody knows she did it."

"That's just it," Jenny said. "She didn't. Our story is about what really happened . . ."

"What's the arc of the character?"

"I beg your pardon?"

"You know, the through line. There's the reveal, sure. But this isn't *Murder, She Wrote*. We're talking three consecutive nights, during Sweeps Week. Think more in terms of *Lonesome Dove*."

"I see what you mean," said Walter. "Although it's not a Western. . . ."

"More situational, sure," said Kurt.

"Right," said Tip. "Comedy, drama, human interest. Like *Cheers*."

"Or *Roseanne*," said Pete.

Tip slapped the tabletop, jarring the pen by Jenny's tablet. "You got it!"

The pen rolled off the table and plopped into the deep-pile acrylic carpet. Jenny wondered if anyone else noticed. Should she pick it up? She gave it a slight kick but it was embedded in the pile, like a crashed missile.

"May I tell you a story?" she said.

"Go."

She cleared her throat in the palpable silence. This, she thought, is it. Ready or not.

"Lisbeth Stewart Borden," she began, "lived with her sister Emma, her father and her stepmother in Fall River, Massachusetts. Andrew Borden, the seventy-year-old father, was a pillar of the community. He owned a bank, some office buildings and real estate. . . ."

"When was all this?" asked Tip, tapping his pen.

"Eighteen ninety-two," said Jenny. So he hadn't read the script, only the coverage. That was no surprise.

"We could shoot on the Universal backlot," said Kurt.

"How much of the town do we see?" asked Tip.

"Not much," Jenny told him. "The house . . ."

"Big house?"

"I don't know what you think is big. Two stories. They lived beneath their means—he was a penny-pincher."

"Go on."

"I'm just trying to lay in a little background here. Anyway, the father and stepmother had been married for twenty-four years. . . ."

"What happened to the first wife?"

"She died. Lizzie never accepted Abby, the stepmother. She called her Mrs. Borden."

"Borden's Milk, right?"

"I don't think so," said Jenny. "Lizzie was afraid that Abby would get him to change the will, leaving more to her. That was what caused the hard feelings. Five years before, Abby talked her husband into buying her half sister a house."

Tip tapped his pen against his teeth. "What kind of house?"

"It doesn't matter. Anyway. So now it's 1892. Emma gets called away. . . ."

"Emma?"

"Lizzie's sister. She goes to visit a girlfriend in

the next town. Lizzie, Abby, the father and
Bridget, the maid, are alone in the house. For a
few days, everybody in the family is sick. Food
poisoning, maybe—they didn't have refrigera-
tors. Then Uncle John comes for a visit. . . ."

She saw Tip's eyes roll ceilingward as his attention drifted. She decided to cut to the chase.

"Picture this. It's the hottest summer in New
England history. No rain all year. The tempera-
ture's rising. It's so hot that—that the birds are
falling out of the trees."

Tip chuckled. "I like that."

I thought you would, she thought.

"No air-conditioning?"

"None."

"Jesus."

"So this particular morning, Abby gets a note
to go visit a sick friend. She leaves the house at
9:30. Uncle John is already gone. Then the father,
Andrew, takes his morning walk into town, to
check on his bank. The maid goes outside to
wash the windows, and Lizzie starts to iron some
handkerchiefs. At 10:30, the father comes home.
Lizzie helps him lie down in the den for a nap,
then goes outside herself, to the barn. . . ."

"What for?"

"It doesn't matter. She eats some peaches, and
goes back to the house. Inside, she finds her
father with his skull split open. One eyeball
hanging out. His blood spattered all—all over the
wall."

"Too violent," said Tip. "Standards and Practices . . ."

"Quick close-ups," said Kurt. "Keep going. This is good stuff."

"She sends the maid to get a doctor. The police come, and the neighbors. Then somebody asks Lizzie if she knows where her mother is. Has she come home yet? Lizzie rushes upstairs—and sees her stepmother dead in her bedroom. Hacked to death with a big blade, a hatchet or an axe."

"No shit!" said Kurt.

For a few seconds, Jenny could have heard a feather fall in the office. Walter gave her a satisfied look. She had done well.

"It was the maid," said Tip. "The father was doing her."

"No," Jenny said. "The neighbors saw her outside the whole time."

"Uncle John," said Kurt.

"I'm afraid not. He had an alibi for every minute of the morning."

"So it has to be Lizzie," Tip said. "There isn't anybody else. Unless they bashed their own brains out."

"There is one person. . . ." Jenny began.

In the corner of the office, a phone buzzed.

"No calls!" said Tip.

Kebrina went to the corner and spoke in hushed tones, then pressed the hold button.

"It's a Mrs. McAmy, for Jennifer Marlow."

I don't believe it, thought Jenny with a sinking feeling. *My mother!* How did she know I was here? She must have called the house, and Lee suspected the truth and told her I might be at Walter's, and then Walter's secretary . . . It was all too humiliating. She wants to know if I brushed my teeth and have clean underwear on. *Damn you, Mother, how dare you!*

"I'll return the call later," she said, straining to regain her composure.

"She says it's urgent."

Jenny caught Kebrina's eye. The other woman must have been able to read the anxiety and despair and took pity on her. When Jenny shook her head a few millimeters, Kebrina understood. She said something into the phone and hung up quickly, then returned to her chair.

Jenny felt a rage growing inside, at her mother, at Lee for giving out any information, at herself for being foolhardy enough to come here and try to pitch their project alone. It was hopeless. They were only tolerating her, she was sure. There was no part in *Liz* for Lindsay Wagner or Jaclyn Smith or Jane Seymour or Meredith Baxter Birney, and Corbin Bernson and Jimmy Smits and Bruce Boxleitner and Timothy Busfield were all too young to play Andrew Borden. Tip and the others aren't interested, she thought. They're humoring me.

The room became even quieter. Tip stopped clicking his ballpoint pen against his teeth. Kurt was not doodling on his pad but actually taking notes, as was Pete. Kebrina sat as straight and attentive as a schoolgirl at an SAT test. Even Walter was watching her like a hawk.

Tip broke the silence.

"So who did it?"

Jenny was glad that she and Lee and Walter had decided to withhold the last five pages of the script. At least that part of the ploy was working. She felt strangely calm, at one with the silence in the eye of a hurricane. She thought of the Suicide Chair. It was a stunt that daredevils and crazy conceptual artists attempted from time to time. One sat in a chair, surrounded by a circle of twenty-two dynamite sticks. On a signal, the sticks were lighted. If they all went off at exactly the same time, the explosion blew out equally in every direction and the artist was safe. But if one or two failed to ignite, he—or she—was sucked out in the firestorm and killed. That had happened a few times. It was why the stunt was so rarely performed. The question in her mind now was, Has it happened yet, and am I safe? Or am I about to self-destruct at any moment in front of a select audience? She could not decide whether or not she was already doomed.

"Who?" she said evenly. "Let me tell you."

"Wait," said Tip. "Tell Dave Edmond and Rip to come in here. I want them to hear this."

Edmond had on tennis shorts and two-hundred-dollar running shoes, with plenty of scars in between. He squinted at Jenny from behind Coke-bottle glasses and snapped his fingers.

"I saw you in that Woody Allen flick, right? You were great! Janet . . ."

She held out her hand, remaining seated. "Jenny Marlow."

"No, that's not it."

"She's the writer," said Tip.

"Writer? She's too pretty to be a writer!" He withdrew his hand and sat, throwing one leg over the edge of the table.

"Where's Rip?"

"Who can say? He went to Sundance last week, and nobody's seen him since."

"She's got a story," said Tip.

"What kind of story?"

"Just listen."

"All right, I'm listening!"

Dave Edmond gave her his full attention for a moment. He was the one she and Lee would have pitched to, if the younger man, Tip, had not been promoted. Seeing them both, she was not sure there was an advantage either way.

"Where was I?" she asked.

"At the reveal," said Kurt.

"Go ahead," said Tip.

"Yeah," said Edmond, "by all means, young lady! I'm all ears!"

He checked the matte-black chronograph on his wrist, monitoring his pulse, no doubt, while calculating how many minutes were left till his next appointment.

Jenny realized that there was no time to waste. She put her head back and considered the ceiling for inspiration. It was as blank as her mind, except for a water stain around the edges of an acoustic tile. The calmness remained, and so did the anger, but she was at peace with it. Even if she failed now, she would know that she had given it her best shot, without Lee. Forgiving herself for her inherent inadequacy was another matter. But somehow, for now, she found the strength to go on.

"Three women and one man are alone in a house in the heat of summer. It's like . . ." She groped for an image that might grab Edmond by the balls. "Like being inside a coed sauna. They feel that they're living in a dream. Except that it's broad daylight outside."

"Do they take their clothes off?"

At last Kebrina spoke up. "Dave, please!"

"Excuse me!"

Jenny continued.

"Twenty minutes later, two of them are dead. There's no motive. No witnesses. Nobody saw anything. There isn't a scrap of evidence, not even the murder weapon, but the police arrest one of the surviving women, put her on trial anyway, and try to crucify her. *Because she's a woman.*

"The press plays it for all it's worth. But after a while, to their surprise, the tide begins to turn. The woman's movement, from Maine to California, from around the world, rallies to her defense. And their voices are heard. *The New*

York Times refuses to say she's guilty. A chorus of voices is heard all the way into the jury room.

"They find her innocent."

"Yea!"

It was Kebrina. She stopped clapping and folded her hands.

"I like it," said Edmond. "You ought to be an actress, honey. With delivery like that . . ."

"I'm not finished," Jenny heard herself saying.

She was shocked but could not stop herself. More words tumbled out, words she had never written down or rehearsed, words that did not come from Lee or from any book. It had to be said. She opened her mouth and a lifetime of frustration rolled off her tongue like gentle thunder.

"This is a docudrama, not one of your cheap-jack 'reality-based' TV movies straight out of the tabloids. It's not a child-custody case, or a romantic triangle, or a story about how hard it is to run with the jet set and not get addicted to cocaine. It's not about possessive moms or two-timing husbands. It's not, in other words, about women as victims.

"It's about women beating the system in spite of the odds. *Your* system. How they tried to punish one woman for nothing more than *being a woman in a male-dominated culture*. And how they didn't get away with it. It's not a tearjerker about her sad life, so that all the housewives in America will cry their little eyes out and be thankful for their big, strong husbands. It's not about 'empowerment.' It's about truth. And justice. And it doesn't pander to white, middle-class women between the ages of nineteen and forty-five, the ones who do the shopping and buy the products that keep your crap on the air. It's for *all* people. And I hope to God you have the guts, once in your lives, to fit something like *that* into your schedule."

She gathered up her things to go. Walter, she noticed out of the corner of her eye, would not look at her.

"Well, everybody?" said Kebrina, her lips working as she struggled not to grin.

Tip was slumped in his chair, deep in ruminative thought.

"Aren't you gonna tell us who did it?" said Edmond.

"I could," said Jenny, "but I won't. Not unless you pay for it."

She stood up.

"Thank you all very much."

And with that she left.

Chapter 7

"I blew it."

"Why do you say that?"

"I was just too nervous without Lee." Jenny twirled some of her spinach pasta onto a fork and realized that she was not hungry. She set it aside at the edge of her plate.

Libby cut the last of her linguine, colored jet-black by octopus ink, into edible lengths and swirled it around, soaking up pesto sauce. "Does he have to be there for everything you do?"

"No, of course not. But it's always been more his project than mine."

"What do you mean? You did the research, you worked up the drafts . . ."

"And he was there to show me how. He's been through this before. All I know is nonfiction."

"Well, you're doing a great job with fiction at the moment," Libby said, "flogging yourself like this. It couldn't have been that bad. Tell me what happened."

Jenny pushed her plate away and considered the busy dining room of Viva La Pasta, where the late lunch crowd still filled many of the tables. She attempted to recapture the scene in Tip's office but her perspective was incomplete, limited to her own point of view. She wished she knew how she had appeared to them. No, on second thought she did not want to know. It was bad enough to relive her subjective memory of the meeting, with her constantly shifting legs and her shaking fingers and the sound of her own voice so strident in her ears.

"It was a nightmare," she said at last. "They started with the usual questions and suggestions, all unbelievably stupid. Lee taught me to accept everything. He always said to pretend to go along, and then to forget what they said as soon as you leave, because they will. But this time, with so much at stake, and no preparation . . . instead of listening and nodding, I started arguing. Can you believe that? I stood up for *Liz*, as if they were criticizing me personally! I must have come off like a first-class bitch."

"Whoa! You don't know that yet. What did your agent say?"

"Walter? Not much. That's a bad sign. Most of the time, he never stops talking."

"Is everything all right?" said a young waiter with an oil-and-vinegar smile. He had appeared over Libby's shoulder, a wraith in a white shirt who floated unseen between the noisy tables, materializing only when and where he was not needed.

"Fine," said Libby. "Bring us some more of those garlic breadsticks, will you?"

He nodded curtly and drifted away.

"First of all," Libby told her, "you did all right. Get that through your head. Men only respect you if you stand up to them. Otherwise they'll steamroll you."

"But I *did* sound like a bitch."

"That's a word invented by men, to describe strong women. If Lee had said the same things, what would they have called him? Tough-minded? A man who knows what he wants? Damn straight they would."

"They weren't all men. One was a girl."

"Girls are females under the age of ten. How old was she?"

"She looked like she hadn't been out of school very long. She took notes. She never smiled."

"What did she say when you finished?"

"She started to clap."

"There, you see?"

"Then she stopped herself. She had a lot of self-control. More than I had."

Libby put her napkin down and leaned across the table so Jenny could hear her above the raucous din. "What exactly did you say?"

Jenny's mind returned to the sparsely furnished office, the echo of her own harsh voice bouncing back at her from the walls. "I told them that Lizzie was a feminist symbol. I can't believe I said that!"

"Why? It's the truth, isn't it?"

"Whether it is or not, they didn't want to hear that. What's on TV now is journalism made to look like drama, with no point of view."

"So? *Liz* is reality-based. . . ."

"It's a dead issue, as far as they're concerned."

"If you believed that, you wouldn't have bothered to pitch it to them in the first place, and you know it."

"I know. We wanted to do a factual reconstruction. Bring it to life, and vindicate someone who was falsely accused. A way of setting the record straight. A true crime story in historical perspective, with the mystery finally solved."

"Did you tell them that?"

"It probably wouldn't have made any difference."

Libby shook her head, her short hair resetting into a layered cap around her face. "They're not dumb. Ask yourself this. Who are all those shitty TV movies made for? *Women.* Women as sacrificial lambs, and women who get even. And you've written the last word on the subject! They'd be crazy not to take it."

"Except that the case doesn't have that kind of closure. She stood up for herself, and in a sense she won, but what did she win?"

"She was covering for the one who did it. She never broke."

"I don't know that noble, enigmatic women are what the networks want. The advertisers . . ."

"Listen to us!" said Libby. "I'm trying to convince you that you did the right thing, and you're arguing that you were wrong. Lighten up on yourself! It'll work out just the way you want it. You'll see."

"How do you know that?"

"I just do, okay?"

"I wish I could believe that."

The waiter rematerialized, a floating head above the crowd.

"Miss Marlow?"

Jenny blinked at him. "Do you mean Mrs.?"

"I have a phone call for a Jennifer Marlow."

"Who . . . ?"

"This way, please."

Jenny left the table at a complete loss. Who would call her here? Who even knew where she was? She glanced back and pantomimed an exaggerated shrug for Libby's benefit.

The phone was at the end of a short hallway, between the cash register and the kitchen.

"Line two," the waiter told her, picking up a

serving of fettucine Alfredo before disappearing again.

"Hello?"

She did not know what to expect. Walter? Lee? She might have mentioned to him that she was having lunch with Libby. But when she heard whose voice it was, her heart sank.

"Jennifer?"

"Mother?"

"Why yes, dear. Can you hear me? You sound so far away!"

"I *am* far away." Two thousand miles, she thought, and then some. "How—how did you know where to reach me?"

"Well, I had to call Information, of course. Lee told me where you were having lunch . . ."

"But Lee doesn't know."

"Then it was that lawyer, what's his name?"

"Walter? You called my agent?" She felt anger but repressed it.

"His secretary, I believe it was. We tried to catch you right after your meeting, but . . . Do you know how many Viva La Pastas there are in Los Angeles?"

The doors to the kitchen flopped open as another waiter squeezed past, balancing a pizza, two Caesar salads, and a plate of mostacelli on his forearm. She turned sideways against the wall.

"Is something wrong, Mother?"

"No, dear . . ."

She fought with herself to remain rational. "Then why did you call me?"

"Why, to find out how your meeting went!"

I don't believe this, Jenny thought.

"I was going to call you tonight," she said coldly.

"Of course you were, dear. But I couldn't wait. It's so exciting! Your own television program . . . How much are they paying you?"

A busboy rattled past with a cartful of dirty dishes, decorated in smears of bright red sauce and hardening cheese, like the stuffing removed from cholesterol-blocked arteries.

"Don't start counting the money just yet."

"How do you mean?"

"I mean they didn't like it." I should have told her when she tried to interrupt the meeting, Jenny thought. If I had, at least I wouldn't be having this conversation now, and I might be able to hold down the two or three bites of food I managed to swallow.

"I don't understand. Why didn't they like it?"

Now Jenny's anger was about to spiral out of control. She removed the receiver from her ear, ready to slam it down. Then two more waiters passed her, single-file, hemming her in against the racks of grated cheese dispensers and cut lemons. She cupped her hand around the mouthpiece and made an enormous effort to lower her voice.

"They just didn't. Tip hated it." Would that satisfy her? It would have to.

"Who's Tip?"

"The new man in charge. Can we talk about this later?"

"Why didn't he like it? Speak up, dear, I can hardly hear—"

"I don't know why! Because they're stupid, all right? What do you care? You've never cared before. I have to go. . . ."

"It's Lee's fault. He's the stupid one, for making you go to that meeting without him!"

"Lee," she said, "is not stupid. I am, for even trying. Let me tell you one thing. If you say a word about this to Lee before I get home, I'll never speak to you again, do you understand?"

"Oh, I understand."

For a second she thought that it was someone else's voice on the other end, that the lines had gotten crossed. But no, it was still her mother. Only now she was using the other voice. The threatening one with the low, rasping tone, the one that had always frightened Jenny.

"I understand that you had a deal, and they broke it. Well, they won't get away with it. We'll get a lawyer. We'll sue—"

"A lawyer is not what I need." What, then? To get away from her accusations. "Stay out of it."

"You need me."

"I don't."

"A girl doesn't need her mother?" The voice changed back. "Why, of course you do! You need me there to help you!"

"Not now."

"That's when you need your mother most, at a time like this! We're best friends, remember?"

No, we're not, Jenny thought. We never were. I only told you that once, after Daddy left, to make you feel good. I don't know if you're any kind of friend to me at all, or if you ever could be. And that's what I need right now, more than anything else: a friend. I don't even know you. Right now I don't know that I want to.

"I have to go now, Mother. Good-bye."

She hung up as the tears started. She wiped them away fiercely and returned to the dining room.

"Don't tell me." Libby was about to start on her tiramisu. "It was your agent. You got the deal."

"No."

Libby saw her friend's face and almost dropped her dessert fork. "Then who was it?"

"My mother." It was all she could do to say it. "She wanted to know how it went."

"She must love you a lot."

"You don't know my mother."

Libby reached across the tablecloth and rested her hand against Jenny's. "She thinks you're her little girl. She always will."

Jenny saw the other woman's hand on hers, the long, tapered fingers, the short, colorless nails, and the way the fingers began to stroke hers, outlining her thumb, the back of her hand, her wrist.

"But you're not, are you?" Libby said. "You're a woman. You need something more."

"I need a friend, Libby."

"You've got one. Don't you know that? And friends help each other. Tell me how, Jenny. I'm here."

"There's nothing you can do."

"I can try. We all can."

"We?"

"My friends are your friends now. They want to help, too."

Last night, Jenny thought. The party—séance, channeling session, whatever it was. The women all so supportive of each other, and all gravitating around the woman in black, what was her name? Rose. A private club that existed behind closed doors, invisible to the rest of society.

"I'm not one of you," Jenny said.

"How can you be sure?"

Jenny withdrew her hand. "I don't know anything for sure, except that I have a husband I'm in love with, who needs me, just as I need him. He's the one I should turn to first."

"Do you think a man can ever really be your friend? You may not find out until there's a crunch, and by then it may be too late."

"I'll have to take that chance."

Libby smiled a knowing, secret kind of smile. "The Sisters can help, Jenny. In ways you know nothing about yet. But you'll see soon enough."

"Is that what they're called, the Sisters?"

Libby nodded. "They've helped me. I had problems, too. A love affair that went wrong. I didn't know where to turn. Then someone told me about the sessions. . . ."

96

"You mean the channeling?"

"Rose doesn't like that word. There are so many frauds in this town, taking money from the rich. Like the one in Malibu, who claims he's in touch with Starfleet Command. People pay him enormous sums—donations, he calls it—and get answers about how to live their lives. It makes them feel better, for a while. Then they come back for another fix, and another. It's a scam."

"And your friend, Rose. She's not like that?"

Libby laughed. "It's not about money. For one thing, none of us *has* any. She does whatever she can to help. She doesn't know where it comes from. The important thing is, it works."

"In what way?"

"My theory is, it's a kind of collective consciousness that speaks for the group, things we don't even know we know. The whole is greater than the sum of parts. That's why they're called the Sisters."

"Why did you bring me there?"

"You needed help."

"Did it show that much?"

"It did last night."

"You can't help me," said Jenny. "It's about Lee, I see that now. Everything that's happened in the last few days . . . He's the one who needs help. I thought I knew how. I tried, and I failed."

"It's about you, too. And you have a support system now. Let the Sisters take care of it."

"How will they do that?"

"I don't know how it works," Libby said, "but

one thing's for sure. Together, we know a lot more than any of us individually. Rose speaks for all of us. If there's a way, it will come through her. Trust in that. We can help you, Jenny—let me prove it to you. You won't be disappointed, I promise."

Tip rode the elevator to Parking Level One.

When the stainless steel doors opened there he was, propped against the rear wall of the compartment, legs spread wide, the soles of his inflatable tennis shoes showing a sure-grip pattern, head back so that he could see out from under the bill of his baseball cap, one hand hooked in the pocket of his jeans and the other cradling the top-grain leather case under his arm, held gently between his Dodgers jacket and his Perry Ellis shirt as protectively as if it were a diplomatic courier's pouch, The pose was studiously casual, arrived at after careful practice; only his eyes were restless and alert, flicking about nervously, unsure whom he might encounter now that the doors were wide open. They were the eyes of a man who scans any room before entering, who always sits with his back to the wall and who waits for others to identify themselves before engaging in a conversation, a player who never plays unless he is sure he can win easily enough to make it seem effortless.

He ambled past the rows of reserved parking spaces, going for the corner, where he had parked his Mercedes 300TE.

Beyond the concrete pillars, a wash of late-afternoon sunlight poured down the exit ramp, dappling the pearlescent paint of a Lexus, the chrome grille of a Jaguar, the tinted windshield of a Porsche. Each appeared to have been sprayed to a dull matte finish, but that was only because of the air from the city outside, where today a Stage One smog alert was in effect; the heaviest layers, containing the greatest concentration of particulate matter, had filtered down the ramp all day and were now trapped beneath the low ceiling, thickening further as they mixed with the exhaust fumes that had collected under the pipes and ducts. The air roiled and eddied, parting before him like a heat mirage. The atmosphere must have been thicker than usual today. The currents had accumulated to suggest a nearly solid shadow that undulated in the corner behind his car.

Was it more than a shadow?

An oscillating siren began to bleat, as his auto alarm signaled a warning.

He stopped.

Under the wailing he heard, or rather felt, the subsonic rumbling of a truck passing somewhere on the street overhead. The thumping of huge tires over the speed bumps in the lot rattled a line of automatic fire extinguisher nozzles in the ceiling. Tip took out his remote control, a small plastic module attached to his key chain, and pressed a button to deactivate the alarm. The wailing ceased abruptly, emitting a final chirp as the circuitry reset and rearmed itself. Then there was an illusion of total silence. It was a temporary deafness brought on by the unexpected burst of high-decibel sound, and yet through it, barely at the threshold of his hearing, a chain clanked. Or was that the clattering of heavy steel as the truck turned out onto the street, receding into the drumbeat of West L.A. traffic?

"Pedro?"

The parking lot attendant did not appear. He should have been able to hear from his kiosk at the top of the ramp. If not, what good was a car alarm?

"Pedro!"

No good at all, and especially not if it went off every time a piece of heavy machinery passed by. And what about the other cars? Tip always chose the corner because it left no room on either side. But if the lot were full and someone squeezed in and parked on the diagonal lines anyway, then opened a door far enough to touch the molding on his Mercedes, any contact would set off the siren. Pedro had never said anything, but if it went off that easily, what was the point? He would have to take his car into the shop and have the security system recalibrated so that it would not respond unless someone tried to force the lock. Otherwise the alarm would blast until Pedro buzzed him in his office to come down and turn it off or the battery went dead. In the meantime he would give the attendant an extra remote module, just in case . . .

Where was Pedro?

Tip started toward the exit ramp, then changed his mind. It was hardly worth the effort. He would drive past the kiosk on his way out, anyway. If Pedro was not there, Tip would have him fired.

He turned back to his car.

The shadow he had noticed before now congealed and took form, rising up behind the trunk.

It was real, after all. A man with close-cropped hair, or was it a man? Hard to see in the dark angle of the corner.

Tip paused a beat, drawing a deep breath, and said, "Can I help you?"

It was one of the homeless, probably. They could be seen hanging around the perimeter of the upstairs lot at night, hunched in doorways, barricaded in the hedges with their stolen shopping carts, sleeping under newspapers on the bench at the corner bus stop. Police swept the area clean every few weeks, but they always came back. Some of them even carried crude signs: HOMELESS VET WILL WORK FOR FOOD or WOMAN & CAT NEED HELP HAVE NOT EAT IN 4 DAYS.

So now they were in the underground garage, as well. They were getting bolder.

"What do you want?"

No answer.

The shape rose higher. It was tall. In one hand was something heavy. A crowbar, a jack handle maybe.

"Get out of here, or I swear I'll call the cops. Stay back! PEDRO!"

It was a bluff. But it might work. The one thing none of them wanted was trouble with the law.

The shape came around the car.

"Tip . . . ?" said a hoarse, gravelly voice.

That threw him. If the person knew his name, then it was not a transient. Or a car thief. Had he miscalculated? For the moment he stood his ground, as the shape shuffled into the open.

Now, in the fuzzy light from the ramp, it was clear that this one was not dressed in rags. The coat was clean, the short hair neat.

"Sorry," said Tip. "I thought you were, you know, messing with my car or something. . . ."

The shape moved closer. One arm came up, but not to shake hands. The fingers were still holding the iron bar, or whatever it was.

"Do I know you?" Tip said. "What do you—?"

The arm went higher. The object froze in the hazy light, outlined clearly now. It was not a bar. The heavy wedge at the end of the handle shone dully. It was something else, something much heavier, with a sharp edge that glinted as it started down, tracing a silver afterimage on the foul air.

Chapter 8

I could open my own TV repair shop, Lee thought.

He hardly knew where to begin. At first, unlocking the garage door, he had thought it was all junk. Now, as his eyes adjusted, he saw that the garage contained a coral reef of old radios and television sets that his father had collected over the years. Some were nothing more than bare chassis long ago gutted for parts. Others were only empty cabinets of molded plastic, wood-grained steel, veneered fiberboard or lacquered hardwood . . .

At the rear of the garage, a jagged line of picture tubes, piled a third of the way to the ceiling; in the corner, an anthill of paper speaker cones, tilted in all directions; on the workbench, mounds of resistors and capacitors and circuit boards; and elsewhere, covering every square inch of the floor, groups of knobs and dials and parts of every description, roughly sorted according to type, as if for recycling. There was a shortwave receiver from the forties, there a pyramid of ancient Philco and Crosley table radios that were older still. Lee identified the console AM-FM-phonograph combination he had listened to as a child, with its green cat's-eye tuning meter on the front. And there was his own RCA portable record player with the leatherette cover, the one he had used to play his 45s as a teenager. And the 8-track from his first car, the one his father had promised to repair before Lee gave up and installed a cassette deck. He had always wondered what happened to those pieces. When he gave them to his father, they disappeared into the black hole of the garage to be fixed. Some eventually reappeared in working order, but most were never heard from again. Now he saw that they had gone to the graveyard of failed audio-video equipment, the place where old radios and TVs went to die.

What should he do? Sell it? To whom? Not much chance of that now. Times had changed, and the bits and pieces here were sadly out of date. Nobody would want them, except perhaps a few flea market or swap meet diehards.

He could have a garage sale, but who would come?

It had not been junk to his father, of course, who cared about such things. There must be others like him, Lee thought. Should he start with the classified ads? Or merely a sign at the curb that said OLD ELECTRONICS PARTS/ INQUIRE WITHIN?

The thought of scavengers prowling through his father's stash, handling and cherry-picking the treasures that might be here and discarding the rest, filled Lee with despair. How would he set the prices? What is a man's life worth at the end? This was all that was left, along with the cartons of ephemera housed in the spare room.

And what of his mother? What had she saved? There had to be heirlooms, lace and linens and china and knickknacks, passed down from her parents and grandparents. Jenny could help him with that. She would know what to keep and what to throw out. . . .

Outside, a breeze blew and dry leaves fell in the driveway, crackling. The sky was dimming slowly but inexorably. Lee felt goose bumps rising on his arms. He sat down with his back to the open garage door and picked up the nearest paper bag. He wanted to see what was here, what it really was, before the light failed completely.

The bag was dusty and browned. Inside was a

jumble of insulated copper wire and a partial roll of lead solder, kinked and dusky as a mass of dried worms. He was not eager to handle it. He set the bag down and reached for an apple crate that appeared to contain the entire print run of *Radio-TV News*. BETAMAX: The Video Tape Recorder Is Here! proclaimed the top cover.

Behind him, the leaves in the driveway crunched, the sound of desiccated bones grinding to dust.

He turned on the stool.

Someone was coming. More leaves broke and scattered. Lee narrowed his eyes to see who it was.

A tall, round-shouldered figure showed beside the house, moving slowly, deliberately. In the falling darkness, with only a strip of twilight remaining in the sky, all he could make out was a black shape without details or features. A heavy foot scraped the cement.

"Who's in there?" said a deep, husky voice.

Lee stood, stubbing his toe on the crate of magazines. There was no room to set his weight securely. In the dwindling light he was not sure where to step. Where was the switch for the bulb over the workbench? The walls were too far away, anyway.

"It's Lee," he said. "Can I help you?"

The scraping continued, coming closer, crossing the threshold.

"Why, hello, Lee," said the deep voice, by now slightly out of breath.

"Is that you, Mr. Bogen?"

"Well, what do you know! Lee! That must be your car out front. . . ."

Lee took a couple of steps, brought his foot down on a bagful of vacuum tubes but kept moving before he could lose his balance. The bulbs popped and wafer-thin shards of glass were reduced to sand under his heel. Then he was teetering at the front of the garage. He tried to steady himself, managing to grasp the edge of the raised door instead of the other man's arm. Mr. Bogen was none too steady on his feet as it was.

"It's been a long time," said Lee. "How are you?"

"Can't complain."

"I came by to see what needs to be done. I don't know where to start."

"Sure am sorry, Lee."

"I know you are. Thanks." Lee helped him with his crutch so that they were both facing the back porch. "Come on in."

"Oh, no . . ."

"Please. I'd like you to. I haven't been inside yet, and it's getting pretty late."

"Well . . ."

"I insist. Come on, Simon. We'll have coffee."

Lee patted Mr. Bogen on the shoulder and pressed him toward the door to the house. He was glad that someone else was here. He did not relish the idea of being alone in his parents' home. It was still too soon.

He keyed open the lock, found the light switch

for the screened-in porch and helped Mr. Bogen up the steps. The man had a hard time because of his crutch but did not say anything.

Lee saw the sink, the washer and dryer, several socks and a pair of his father's undershorts folded on the counter. He could not bring himself to touch these things as he entered. He remembered where the kitchen light switch was located and went though to the dining room, noting a few cups and saucers still in the dish drainer, waiting to be put away. His mother had washed up before they left that last time, as she always did. The kitchen was spotless. It was her way.

The kitchen bulb cast a wedge of light across the table in the dining room, enough for now. He pulled back a chair for Mr. Bogen and propped the crutch against the wall.

"I'll see if I can find the coffee."

"No need. It's bad for my nerves."

"Me, too," said Lee. He hesitated between the kitchen and dining room, unsure about what to do next.

"Sit," said Mr. Bogen. "Glad you came by. I wanted to talk to you about something."

The air in the house was stale and tinged with the scent of his mother's dish soap and furniture polish. It was a combination he remembered from childhood; breathing it in, he would know that he was home even in total darkness. Now he noticed an additional odor that he could not place, a musty underlay that was also familiar. It was the old carpet, perhaps, or the bedclothes in the other room, a mold under the bathroom sink because of the slowly dripping faucet that his father had never fixed, the composite smell of a place so long lived-in that it has absorbed the very essence of its long-term occupants, the secretions of their skin and the oils in their hair and the breath in their lungs, the irreducible nature of their beings. Ventilating the house would never change that. It was in the wallpaper, the floorboards, the upholstery and the furniture in every room, and the house would retain it forever. They had left behind their watermark and it would remain even if the house were demolished, in the piles of debris exposed to the elements, hanging over the lot like a cloud of radiant energy that would not go away, a radioactive residue with an infinite half-life. No, not quite infinite. That would be a denial of life itself. Nothing that lives is permanent. That was its beauty and its triumph. That was what made it so precious.

Now Lee felt unsteady, as if his legs were melting out from under him and dissolving into the shadows of the dining room. He felt for the back of a chair and seated himself.

"I don't know where to start," he said again.

"Well, you could sell," Mr. Bogen told him, "or rent it out. If you want to deal with that. I have a cousin who can help, if you want some advice."

"I just might take you up on that." Now that Lee was seated, he felt resigned to the weight settling over him. "As soon as I decide. I don't know where their papers are, if they had a safe-deposit box . . . I don't even know if they left a will."

"That's for the lawyers to sort out. You have other things to worry about."

I don't know if they had a lawyer, either, Lee thought. The information would be with their papers. In the small drawer in the bedroom? That was where she had kept his report cards and the Indian head pennies from his grandmother. . . .

"Thank you," said Lee. "I'm glad you came by, too. You were the best friend they had, for a lot of years. . . . It will take me a while to sort things out. But I'll get it done. I'm not worried about it."

"That's not what I mean." The old man looked away, unable to meet Lee's eyes but determined to do his duty.

"What *do* you mean?"

"Something I was going to tell you." Lee saw the man's lips twitch. "It's nothing, I guess. . . ."

"No, please. Go ahead."

"I'm a busybody, sticking my nose in other people's business. . . ."

"Tell me what, Simon?"

"Well, I just got to wondering . . ."

"Say it."

"Wondering who it was that night."

Lee was aware of a cold pressure in his chest, wrapping itself around his heart. "You mean the night before the accident?"

"I couldn't sleep. I can't most nights. It's this leg. All the years I had it, I never gave it any thought, but since they took it off, well, it keeps me awake. I get shooting pains. Like it's still there. . . ."

Get to the point, Lee thought. "Who did you see?"

"Well, I was up watching TV. I always leave the lights off, so I won't disturb anybody. It must have been three-thirty, four in the A.M. I heard . . ."

"A car?" said Lee.

The old man looked at him sideways. "How did you know?"

"I thought you said it was a car."

"I didn't. But it was. Stopped down the block, by the Lehmans'. When you're retired, you notice things. Little things in the neighborhood, you know? So I looked out. The Lehmans' place was dark, all right. But there was a car in front."

"What kind of car?"

"Couldn't tell. Then somebody comes along on the sidewalk. I had to see where they were going, for the Neighborhood Watch. We're supposed to report anything. . . . Anyway, they come right up to Jerry and Adrienne's. She doesn't go to the front door. . . ."

"She?"

"Well, I couldn't swear to it, but I'd have to say female. The walk . . . there are ways to tell."

"What did she do?"

"Nothing. She stands there on the sidewalk, reading something off a piece of paper. The address, maybe. But she doesn't go up and knock. You know what she does?"

Lee was afraid that he knew what Mr. Bogen would say next.

"Where was their car?" he asked.

"Parked in front. Like always."

"I knew it."

"You did?"

"Go on."

"Well, this person, instead of ringing the doorbell, she goes to the car. Their car. She checks her piece of paper again, and the license plate. Then she disappears."

"What do you mean?"

"For a minute I can't see her, 'cause she's bent down in front of the car. Then she shows her face, to be sure nobody's looking. I am, but she doesn't know it. . . .

"The next thing I see, her feet are sticking out—she's down on her knees. Got a flashlight. She's looking for something under the front of the car. Or doing something. I don't know which. . . .

"After a while, she gets up and walks back down the street. Gets in her car, and drives away. That's it."

"Did you see the license plate?"

"Too far away."

"What about her face?"

"Never saw her before in my life. Short hair. Little eyes."

"Would you know her if you saw her again?"

"Might. Might not. It was dark." Mr. Bogen leaned across the table and showed Lee both sides of his face. His eyes were bulging. "What I want to know is, Why would somebody be messing around with your dad's car like that? You have any idea?"

Lee said, "I'm afraid I do."

When Jenny got home, the phone was ringing.

At first she was not sure where the sound was coming from. She unlocked the deadbolt and entered the darkened living room as the chirping continued. For a moment she thought a bird was trapped under the glass tabletop by the couch, flapping its wings. She saw a single red eye, tiny as a surgical laser beam, shining at her. Then she touched the lamp switch, and saw that it was the LED in the telephone handset, lying on the table exactly where she had left it hours ago. The red light pulsed with every ring.

"Lee?" she called out. "Are you home?"

No answer.

She crossed the room and snatched up the phone.

"Hello?"

"Have you seen the news?"

"The news?" A man's voice. Not her husband's, but familiar. "Why?"

"Turn on your TV."

"Walter, is that you? I just got home. What . . . ?"

"Tip's dead."

"I don't understand what you're saying."

"Just turn it on."

She pressed the remote control and the television set blipped on. "Walter, what—?"

"Somebody killed him in the parking lot this afternoon."

"You've got to be kidding."

"You know me better than that."

The picture tube flickered on and a blurry, low-contrast image came into focus, accompanied by a soundtrack of screaming voices and bodies in motion. It was MTV. She pressed the channel selector and held it down, as a montage of automobile and restaurant commercials flashed by. Walter was still speaking.

"What did you say? I can't hear you. Wait." She hit the mute button and suctioned the handset against her ear.

"It happened a couple of hours after we left his office. Probably an attempted carjacking. When he tried to stop the guy, Tip got his head bashed in."

She found the Eyeball News channel and left it there. Just now the female newscaster was smiling unabashedly into the camera, her eyes twinkling, as a chroma-keyed shot of a little girl with braces on her legs filled the bluescreen behind the reporter's head.

"Little Amy left the hospital for the first time in three years, and spent the day at the Happiest Place on Earth. . . ."

"Does Lee know?" Walter was saying.

"I don't think so. I just walked in."

"When he gets there, have him call me."

"Why don't you just tell me, Walter? Is there something more? There is, isn't there?" She touched the mute button again. "You don't have to say it. *Liz* is dead, isn't she? I killed her. Well, I'd like to be the one to tell Lee, if you don't mind."

"What are you talking about?"

"The meeting, Walter. The way I blew it."

"I wouldn't say that."

"Talk to me the way you talk to Lee, all right? I saw their eyes. They looked at me like I was trying to sell them a sack of shit."

"Don't jump to conclusions. . . ."

"Don't humor me, Walter. This isn't a joke!"

"I never joke."

She thought of Walter's long, craggy face, the drooping eyes, and knew that he was right. No attempt at humor had ever passed his lips. He was a show business agent.

"The police are taking statements," he continued. "I'm going down in the morning. Did they call you yet?"

"I haven't played back my messages."

"If they call, you don't know anything about it."

"You're right, I don't!"

"Just tell them that. It's a formality. Meanwhile, no statements to the press. It'll be all over the trades tomorrow, anyway. Let me handle everything. Tell Lee to stop mourning and get it together. I can book him on *Entertainment Tonight*, *Hard Copy* . . ."

"Walter, you're sick, do you know that?"

"I'm a pragmatist. That's what you have to be now, too. Get Lee in shape for the interviews. . . . 'Producer of axe-murder telefilm found hacked to death. Now meet the writers!' You can't buy a press release like that!"

She cut him off. "That's enough. Lee will talk to you when he's ready. Are your parents living, Walter?"

Or don't you have any? she thought.

He ignored her question. "We'll talk later," he said, and hung up.

On TV, little Amy was surrounded by midgets in animal suits with huge round ears and furry hands; she cowered under the pressure of their monstrous eyes and hebephrenic grins. Jenny shuddered and left the sound off. She set the phone down on the table and scanned the rest of the L.A. stations. There was a sportscaster, there a stock market report, there a weatherman pointing to an animated map. Precipitation loomed on the horizon.

Now meet the writers, she thought with disgust. Had Walter really said that? Or was it *writer*? *Tell Lee . . . Get Lee . . . I can book him on . . .* It was as if she did not exist. Even if I wanted to be a part of his publicity scheme, which I don't. They stick together, don't they? The Men's Club.

The telephone chirped again.

"Lee?" she said hopefully.

"Jenny, are you all right? I just saw the news."

"Libby, I cannot believe this!"

"Stay where you are. I'm coming over."

116

"No, please." Libby sounded more than sympathetic, and yet there was a detachment in her voice that confused Jenny even further. "There's nothing more you can do. I mean there's nothing *to* do . . . Libby, I've been trying to remember. What did your friend, the medium, say last night?"

"Rose isn't a medium. She's a trance-channeler."

"Something about a blade . . ."

Jenny was getting a very peculiar feeling in her stomach. It was even greater than the anxiety she had learned to live with lately. Something was taking shape inside her, an awareness that she could not name. There were no words for the feeling yet, only the tingle of a dawning awareness. That was a warning. She had to do something about it now, before it got any stronger.

"I don't remember," Libby said.

"But I need to know."

"The only thing you need to know is that it doesn't matter now *what* Tip thought. You can go on to any other producer in town—you're free! There are plenty out there who will understand what you wrote. In the long run, you're better off."

There was a pause on the line, an empty space that began to fill with hisses, as if someone or something else were gaining strength, feeding and drawing energy from the phone lines, about to make its message known.

"Libby, *what the hell is going on?*"

"I think you'd better talk to Rose about that."

"I don't want to talk to Rose. I'm talking to you. I thought you were my friend."

"I am, but I'm not the channel. We can call a session tonight, if you—"

"Let's cut through all this," said Jenny. "What do you know about what happened today?"

Onscreen, roughly edited footage of an office building. A male reporter in an off-the-rack sport coat and striped tie spoke earnestly into the camera. Behind him, several squad cars blocked the ramp to the underground garage, the same one Jenny and Walter had used earlier in the day.

"What do you mean?" said Libby. "We were trying to help you, that's all."

"Help me how?"

"How do you think? Jenny, what are you asking me?"

Jenny tapped the remote control, easing the sound up in small steps until she could hear what the reporter was saying in the background. It was basic. The police had made no arrests yet and had no clues. It all sounded so mundane, as if murders happened here every day. And in fact they did.

"I don't know what I'm asking. Forget it."

"Jenny, you're upset. Let the Sisters help you. I'll pick you up. . . ."

"Help me *how*? Will you just tell me that?"

"I don't understand it any more than you do."

"Don't you?"

"It works—that's all that matters, isn't it? If a message came through for you, the choice is

yours as to whether or not you want to heed it."
Libby drew a breath and there was more hissing
on the line. "We'll drive to Silverlake . . ."

"Don't come over."

"Why not?"

"I'm waiting for Lee." He'll know what to do,
she thought.

"Don't you get it? He doesn't understand you!
He's wrapped up in his own problems . . ."

"His problems are mine, too. He's my husband."

Was the crackling on the line a stifled laugh?

"Jenny, who am I? Do you know who you're
talking to?"

"You're my friend. We're friends, all right? But
that's all I need from you. Not anything else."

"You think I'm trying to put the make on you?
If I were going to do that, it would have happened a long time ago. A long, long time."

"I don't mean that."

"Then accept my help. You're upset. What are
friends for?"

The headache was back. It stabbed her
between the eyes, so sharply that she almost
cried out in pain. "I'm sorry. I don't know what
I'm saying. I'll call you later. . . ."

"Promise?"

Jenny broke the connection with a trembling
fingernail.

*"The victim has been identified as Stanley 'Tip'
Topp, the producer of such popular television pro-
grams as* Watusi: the Story of a Dance, Don't

Take My Child! *and Michael Jackson's award-winner,* Diana Ross: A Life Supreme. . . ."

Though the phone was off, the red light blinked at her. That meant the battery was low. She carried it with her to the downstairs bathroom, found her pain pills in the medicine cabinet, swallowed two dry and went on to the kitchen.

She hung the phone on the wall to recharge, then noticed the answering machine on the counter. A red light was blinking there, too. That meant there had been several calls while she was out. Should she be grateful that Lee had thought to turn it on before he left? She hoped so.

With some trepidation she pushed the automatic rewind button and waited for the replay.

The first message began with the sound of static on the line.

"Jennifer, this is your mother. I want to know how your meeting went! I'll call again in a while, when you're home . . ."

Thank you, Mother, Jenny thought. What difference does it make to you? It's not your series, is it?

The second message began with another whisper of white noise.

"Don't you worry, darling. If they don't want your script, well then, that's their loss! They'll be sorry . . ."

She fast-forwarded and released the switch for the start of the third message.

"You shouldn't have trusted Lee and that shyster

agent. . . . *Why didn't you listen to me? They don't know what this means to us! They're not family . . . !"*

As the fourth message began, she became aware that something was wrong with the tape. Her mother's voice dropped an octave to a lower, throatier pitch. Then she realized that it was not the fault of the machine. The voice actually was deep and husky, almost masculine.

"No, you wouldn't ask for help! You thought you could do it all yourself. But you couldn't, could you? I blame you for this, Jennifer. For not turning to me. I tried to tell you, but you wouldn't listen. A girl should listen to her mother. You should know by now that I'm your best friend. . . ."

The machine rolled on. Jenny was not able to turn it off. She listened with an appalled fascination.

"I'm going to help you, Jennifer, whether you like it or not. I'm coming to be with you. . . ."

"No!" Jenny said.

". . . and to help you close the deal. You'll see. If you can't do it on your own, if you're so pigheaded, so incompetent, then I'll show you . . . !"

Chapter 9

From the end of the block, the town houses and condominiums were black and jagged against the sky.

Lee thought of the Griffith Park Planetarium, where he had gone for field trips as a boy; there the false horizon around the curvilinear wall was a cut-out diorama of a suburban skyline at sundown. But the silhouette he now saw through his windshield was not generic. The largest condos jutted up severely behind the security fence, roofs with unexpectedly sharp angles, even the occasional satellite dish. There were tall pine trees with conical tops pointed spearlike at the first star of evening, there a high hedge that could have been the boundary of a maze, and there a sentinel line of giant palms swaying under the moon. He had never noticed until now just how baroque the complex was with its looming asymmetry, next to the conventional housing developments on either side. If this was its true shape, then it only showed itself by night.

Lee suppressed the feeling and turned down to the protected garage, then entered his code on the keypad and waited for the gate to open . . .

Ed Lawseth, his parents' mechanic for so many years, had checked their car thoroughly the day before the accident. It was something he did every time Jerry and Adrienne took a trip. New plugs and radiator hoses, air filter and oil change, even a brake inspection. The man was adamant. There had been nothing wrong with the car.

At least not until the next morning.

What could have caused the brakes to fail? Ed had no idea. In fact he said flatly that it was impossible, unless someone had tampered with the lines.

And it was apparent now that someone had.

Sometime during the night—about three A.M., if Simon Bogen was right. Lee had no reason to disbelieve their neighbor. The accident only confirmed his suspicions. An unknown saboteur had parked out of sight up the street, walked quietly to the Buick at the curb and, working under cover of darkness, made a small cut in each of the brake lines leading from the master cylinder. Not all the way through, but enough to cause the pressurized fluid to leak out after a few miles.

A woman?

Lee found that part hard to swallow. But whoever it was had an easy job. The Buick was always parked outside, since his father had turned the garage into a makeshift workshop and storage area. They did not even park it in the driveway; Lee's mother worried about oil spots on the cement.

It was barely a lead, but it was all he had.

Mr. Bogen had not seen a license plate and could not even provide a meaningful description for the police. If the police would be interested. Which was not likely. It seemed that their prime directive was something other than the pursuit of justice. It was their job to make arrests on demand, to provide closure for society following a crime. But what if neither society nor the police noticed that a crime had been committed?

The gate opened, and he swung the car down the ramp.

The first problem would be convincing the police that there had been sabotage. For them to admit the possibility meant opening up one more investigation. Why should they bother? They had their version of the event. An elderly couple lost control of a vehicle and went off the road. A heart attack or stroke; who knows? who cares? Why go looking for a crime when there was already a perfectly reasonable explanation?

So Lee would have to solve this on his own.

He could go back to Mr. Bogen again, with a tape recorder, in case the man remembered any further details. He could interview the other neighbors; maybe someone else had seen the woman in black, too. He could take possession of the brake assemblies with the cut hydraulic lines, for evidence. He could check his parents' letters and papers, to see if they had any enemies. As unlikely as that was. . . .

He slipped into his parking space at the far wall of the security garage.

Most of the other spaces were filled, now that the residents were home for the evening. There was Jenny's car next to his. He opened his door carefully; the way she was parked, with the concrete pillar on one side and only his space on the other, she would know where any new dings or scratches came from. He locked his car and headed for the stairs that led up into the walled complex.

There was work to be done here, too, even if he turned the whole thing over to a private investigator. He needed to check on the wreath of black roses. It should be easy enough to locate the florist who filled the order and made the delivery. Perhaps the clerk would remember who placed it. There couldn't be that many requests for dead flowers. And there was the wreath itself. Jenny had thrown it out, but was she absolutely certain that it contained no card or other clue?

With any luck it would still be in the Dumpster.

He came up into the grounds near the rec room. Inside, two young men with short hair and baseball caps were playing Ping-Pong. As he passed, the ball went wide and struck the soft drink machine in the corner, then bounced away into the shadows. The young men laughed hoarsely. Lee did not recognize them, and walked on.

No one was in the pool tonight, at least not that he could see. The weather had turned and there was a breeze in the trees and shrubbery, shaking the branches gently but gaining momentum. Was a storm coming? He had not bothered to watch the news for several days. Now the surface of the water rippled, as if something were thrashing at the near side of the pool, under the concrete lip, sending out shock waves. Were the waves getting stronger? He glanced through the wrought-iron bars of the gate and saw only empty deck chairs, a forgotten towel and a stained life preserver. He kept walking.

He could almost make out his house from here. It was on the far side of a grove of Dutch elms that ran parallel to the stone path. At right angles to the path was a row of condos, these only single-story, attached units, and beyond them a building containing two-room studio apartments that the owners subleased to students from the community college. He and Jenny had bought the last of the two-story model homes of the western perimeter, with a patio, a small backyard and a functional balcony. It was better than renting until they could find and furnish a proper house. That would depend on their income, of course. *Liz* would be their ticket out. Meanwhile this was a way of establishing credit. . . .

Was there a light in his upstairs window?

It might have been a reflection from one of the lampposts along the path. He stopped walking and waited for another glimpse through the moving branches of the elm trees.

The breeze touched each tree before passing on. He saw finally that the white circle in the window was the round face of the moon, cut across with thin strands of drifting fog so that the face appeared to be wrapped in a flowing white scarf. He could not see the first-floor windows from here. Another breeze entered the grounds from the east, this one forceful enough to shake leaves down onto the path.

Jenny.

He wanted to be home, to see her. She had been so supportive during these difficult days, even meeting with Walter and perhaps the network underlings on her own, without him, if he knew her as well as he thought he did. He was sure she had done well. If anything she knew the material better than he did, and she was quicker on her feet. He wanted to hear how it had gone, and to hold her in his arms and tell her that he was through grieving. He would get back to the negotiations tomorrow, along with his investigation. There was no reason to say anything more about the accident for now. That would only make her more nervous than she already was. As soon as they got their deal, he would explain everything. By then he might have enough answers to start making sense.

He neared the last of the elm trees, and the path that led to his house.

A hundred feet or so farther, another path led down to the trash bins behind the buildings.

Was the wreath still there?

Once he was inside with Jenny, it would be hard to find an excuse to leave again. But it would be on his mind. He would be thinking the whole time about those damned blackened roses.

His footsteps echoed around him, reflected off the facades of the town houses.

He slowed, considering which fork to take.

The sound of his footsteps did not slow.

He stopped.

The footsteps continued on at an even pace.

He looked back. The path was empty, except for the regularly spaced circles of light from the lampposts.

He looked ahead.

And saw a large shadow fall across the front of his house, spreading like an inkblot.

The sound of the footsteps came closer.

From far down the smaller path, someone was approaching. A security spotlight threw a silhouette against his house, magnified to several times its normal height. Lee could not tell who it was, only that the figure appeared to be very tall, moving with a shambling gait.

The silhouette had something in its hand. Something long and thin, with a sharp wedge at the end.

Lee could have turned away. He could have gone up the sidewalk to his home and let himself in.

Instead he waited.

As the figure shifted course, Lee caught the full glare of the spotlight behind it and was temporarily blinded. He shielded his eyes.

"Señor Marlow?"

It was the gardener.

"Hello, Paulino," said Lee. "Working late, huh?"

Paulino paused, and the footsteps stopped. He brandished a shovel.

"The dogs," he said. "They sneak in again, for the garbage cans. I clean up their mess. . . . Señora Marlow told me of your sad news." He came closer, touching his chest. "I am very sorry."

"Thank you, Paulie."

"It is a terrible thing."

"Yes." He looked past Paulino, down to the end of the smaller path, where the Dumpsters were. "Listen, do you know if the trash men have been here?"

"Trash men?"

He tried to remember what day it was. "Do they still come on Saturday?"

"Oh yes, Saturday. Tomorrow. You have something for me to carry?"

"No, that's all right. I was just wondering. Good night."

"Good night, Señor Marlow."

As soon as Paulino was gone, Lee went down to the Dumpsters.

There were only two steel bins. The sides were battered and dented, as if something large and powerful had been trapped inside under the heavy lids and had kicked the interior walls repeatedly, struggling to get out.

He lifted the first lid and peered inside.

Except for a layer of mottled newspapers on the bottom, the Dumpster was empty.

He opened the second one.

It, too, was filled with nothing but darkness. Lee smelled the lingering stench of garbage and dropped the lid. It clanged hollowly, nearly catching his fingers and flattening them into pulp.

How could the bins be empty? Tomorrow was pickup day. Paulino had said so.

Lee remembered now. There were always several bins here. That meant the full ones were already outside at the curb, ready for tomorrow morning, when the sanitation trucks would hook them with their forklifts.

That was where the wreath was, in one of the full Dumpsters outside the complex.

He followed the grooves in the cement, where

the heavy Dumpsters were wheeled out once a week through an access gate used only by the maintenance crew.

The gate was locked.

Lee found a pressure plate in the cement, where a sensor was embedded below the surface. When a car or truck—or the Dumpsters, presumably—rolled over it, the weight sent a signal to open the access gate.

He stepped on it, rocking back and forth, but his weight was not enough to complete the circuit.

Well, he thought, that's it. Either I climb over the fence, or I go all the way back to the main entrance and walk around the block. . . .

Then he saw the control box. It was mounted on a short pole to the left of the driveway, so that Paulino and the other workers could open the gate manually from the inside, if necessary.

Lee found a button and pressed it.

The iron gate creaked and began to slide open.

The other Dumpsters were at the curb.

He went to the first one and pried the lid up a few inches. As it lifted, the smell was overpowering. A stinking clot of garbage and trash moldered inside, coffee grounds and eggshells and rotten vegetables and God only knew what else.

If the wreath was here, buried under the decomposing mass, he would never find it.

As he moved to the next Dumpster, a car passed on the street, catching him in its headlights.

"Hey!"

The car slowed. A cop, probably. What must I look like? A bum scrounging for discarded food. I'll tell him I'm looking for my wife's wedding ring. She dropped it in the wastebasket and—

"Lee? Is that *you*?"

He knew the voice.

He took his hand away from the lid and faced the street. A Porsche 944 hovered at the opposite curb. The passenger window was down and a familiar face was leaning across the seat, glowering at him.

"Hi, Walter."

"How the hell do I get in? I've gone around the block three times. . . ."

Walter had never been here before. But he had decided to stop by tonight. That must mean he's got some news, Lee thought. It's good news, or he would never have left the comfort of Marina del Rey.

Lee motioned toward the service driveway.

"Over here."

The headlights swept the gate as the car made a J-turn.

The gate was already closing after Lee's exit. He watched, unable to stop it. Walter's car nosed into the driveway and idled noisily as the bars clanged shut.

"Would you mind opening it?" said Walter gruffly.

"I can't," Lee said. He pointed to an electronic keypad outside the gate. "I don't know the code."

"You don't? How long have you lived here?"

"I use a key. Anyway, this is the service entrance."

"What if you don't have your key?"

"Then I punch in the residents' code. But it's only for the parking lot."

"You're sure about that, are you?"

Lee tried the only numbers he knew. They did not work. He looked at the tinted windshield, at the approximate area where he thought Walter would be, and held out his arms in a helpless gesture.

Walter gunned the engine and backed out, screeching to a halt in the street. Then he jack-knifed the car around and tucked it against the curb. He got out, slammed the door and immediately used his beeper to arm the car's antitheft device.

"We have to talk," he said.

"What about?" Lee started walking. It was too much to ask Walter to disarm the car alarm, get back in and drive them both to the front of the complex. This would give them a chance to have their talk, anyway. "Come on. I'll show you—"

"Are the police here yet?"

"Police?"

"I thought I'd better come by. . . . Haven't you seen the news?"

"Not yet."

"Jenny didn't tell you?"

"I just got here myself. What are you talking about, Walter?"

"My God. You really don't know."

"Know *what*?"

"Where are we going?"

"To the front gate. Walter—"

"We'd better talk about this inside."

"Don't fuck with my head, all right? I can't take it tonight. Now what—?"

"Tip's dead."

"Who?"

"The new V.P. in Charge of Programming. He was murdered this afternoon. It was like something out of a goddamn horror movie. . . ."

Jenny rewound the tape and her mother's voice became a high-pitched chattering. In reverse it sounded even less human. She shuddered and reset the answering machine. Soon the voice would be erased as new messages replaced the old, messages she wanted to hear.

Unless her mother called again.

She pressed the OFF button and the red monitor light winked out.

There, she thought. That will stop her. I can't take any more of her psychotic ramblings. Not now. Maybe not ever again.

She left the kitchen and went down the hall to the living room.

Outside, it was already dark. That was almost comforting. It meant that the day, this grotesque sequence of events might finally come to a close.

She did not need to turn on the lamp. The stairway was directly ahead, to the right of the fireplace. For now, she wanted to go upstairs and peel off her clothes and take a scaldingly hot shower. That was all.

No, not all. . . .

Lee, where are you?

There was no way to reach him. She did not know where he had gone. Probably to his parents' house in Pasadena to sort things out. If so, he would be even more depressed tonight.

She could try calling him there.

No, let him do what he needs to do.

Come home, she thought. We'll crawl into bed together and start fresh in the morning. A new beginning. Things will be clearer then. Just come home.

Now.

She climbed the stairs easily in the semi-darkness and entered the bedroom. She undressed quickly and crossed to the bathroom and reached out for the light switch on the wall, when she heard a movement in the vicinity of the bed.

She froze.

"Is anybody there?" she said too loudly.

No answer.

Of course not. It was absurd. If someone were hiding in the room, an intruder, a burglar, he was not about to announce himself. An animal, then? A bird? She had not left a window open. And the flue in the fireplace was closed, she was sure.

A mouse. Or worse, a rat. . . .

She flipped the light switch.

And saw a clawed hand outside the second-floor window. As she watched, it scratched repeatedly at the glass, trying to get in.

It was only the elm tree. The end of a long, crooked branch swayed as the breeze outside became a wind, and a small, gnarled twig moved like a crooked finger, beckoning her to the window.

She tiptoed across the carpet in her bare feet and looked out.

The horizon was black and invisible against the sky; only the branch was illuminated by the spill of light from the bathroom. Below, rows of trees swayed and shook, separating this house from the rest of the grounds. At regular intervals along the path soft, misty lampposts could be seen between the trees.

Was that a dark, hunched figure walking slowly from one circle of light to the next?

She stood closer to the window, then drew back, startled, as her breasts made contact with the glass. There was the silhouette of her body reflected in the pane, edged in yellow light from across the room. Only one side of her face was visible, the other half in shadow, with a lingering residue of condensation where her mouth should have been. Mist still clung to the glass, fogged by her breath.

She focused through her own translucent reflection. Whoever had been on the path was gone now. Or had she only disappeared momentarily into the darkness between the lampposts?

She?

Why did I think that? It could be a man, couldn't it?

She stepped back from the window, suddenly aware of her nakedness.

He can see me, she thought.

She crossed her arms over her chest and shivered.

Then she closed the drapes, and went to take her shower.

By the time she finished and turned off the water, steam filled the bathroom, occluding the mirror, dripping in rivulets down the walls, billowing out in a low mist over the bedroom carpet.

Above the final trickling of the shower nozzle, she heard a distant buzzing, like an insect attempting to communicate.

She shook the water out of her ears, but it did not go away.

She wrapped a towel around her head, slipped into her terry-cloth robe and leaned out into the bedroom. A fog rolled out before her, gathering at her ankles, white as ectoplasm against the darkness.

The buzzing came from somewhere downstairs, she realized.

The intercom by the front door. It had to be. That meant someone was outside the complex, calling her house to be let in.

It could be Lee.

She left her slippers to the shadows under the bed.

Before she got downstairs, the buzzing stopped.

She hurried through the living room, cursing when her knee struck the edge of the table. Where was the lamp? She lunged for the intercom, found the button and leaned close.

"Yes?"

All that came out of the speaker was white noise.

She held the button down.

"Is anybody there?"

Too late. She gave up, backed away and fumbled in the darkness for the lamp. There it was.

She was about to click it on, when she heard someone approaching on the walkway outside.

She waited, listening to the footsteps.

They did not pass by. Instead they stopped, hesitated and then started again. Growing louder. Coming this way.

"Lee," she whispered.

She waited for his key to scratch at the lock.

Instead the doorbell rang.

Lee would have used his key. At the front gate, as well.

She was not ready to deal with anyone else. She stood very still. If she left the light off, whoever it was would assume that no one was home and move on.

The bell rang again.

Standing in the dark, feet wet, steam rising from her legs, she did not know what to do.

There was a long pause.

The footsteps did not go away.

Then someone knocked on the door.

For reasons she did not consciously understand, her heart began to beat faster. Her temples throbbed. She felt a tightening behind her eyes and the first sharp jab of pain at the center of her forehead.

The knocking became a pounding fist.

All right! she thought. Anything to stop the pounding.

"Who is it?"

"Jenny?" said a muffled voice.

It sounded familiar.

She grasped the knob, unhooked the chain and opened the door. At the same time the wind gusted. The door blew out of her hand and banged against the wall.

With the wind in her eyes, it was hard to see who was there. She forced her eyelashes apart and felt her skin go cold under the robe as the air rushed up under it, encircling her body in an icy grip.

When she opened her eyes, a figure was standing there on the porch, a silhouette against the lamppost opposite the house. The shape seemed thick, massive, with wild spikes of hair flaying madly away from its skull.

Then the shape spoke.

"Let me in!" it said.

Chapter 10

At the front gate, Lee punched in the directory number to buzz his own house, as if he were a visitor.

"So use your key," said Walter. "You have one, don't you?"

"Sure. I just wanted to let Jen know I'm home." *I want to hear her voice,* he thought. Somehow that was very important to him just now.

"She probably went out." Walter scraped the soles of his baby crocodile loafers on the jute mat outside the main entrance to the complex. "I talked to her a couple of hours ago, after it went down."

There was no response. Lee gave up on the buzzer and dug in his pocket for the keys. "What happened, Walter?"

"Tip got his head caved in by a carjacker. That's what the police say."

"I mean before. At the meeting." Lee aimed his key at the gate.

"That's what's so ironic. . . ." Walter stopped Lee's hand and pushed the gate. It swung open. "Some security."

Someone had failed to pull it shut all the way. The hinges were spring-loaded, but sometimes a resident left it ajar long enough to check the mailboxes. This time there was no one in sight. Lee held the gate for Walter, then locked it firmly behind them.

"I thought it was Dave Edmond's decision."

"It was, till Tip came aboard."

"It's just as well I wasn't there," Lee said flatly. "The way I feel, I would have blown it."

"Jenny thought she did," said Walter, following him through the underpass and along the flagstone path.

"Did she? What did she say?"

"You should have heard her. She laid it on them. The network is full of shit, everything they know is wrong. A speech!"

"That doesn't sound like Jen," said Lee.

The path took them around the pool. "You're damn right it doesn't! Whatever got into her, I say we all need some of that. She read them the fucking riot act. Then she walked out. It was so quiet you could hear everybody's ulcers bleeding. . . ."

As they walked the path from one circle of light to another, the wind at their backs, Lee saw the progression of his life stretched out before him: a journey interrupted from time to time by brief bright spots before leading inevitably into darkness again. Darkness was the norm, with the bright moments few and far between and no guarantee that you would ever make it to the next one; and if by some miracle you did, there was the certainty that it would not last. The wind shook the trees, rearranging the leaves into patterns that warned of unknown and undefined dangers. One must stick to the path regardless, he thought. It was the only possible hope.

"So," Lee said, "we go to another network and start over. Fox?"

"Are you kidding? They loved it! Tip and Dave Edmond both! They gave it the green light!"

Now, hearing the news he had waited so long for, Lee should have felt the sweet rush of victory. Instead he felt nothing.

"I talked to Dave an hour ago. He wants *Liz* to kick off the new season, the Big Event for Sweeps Week. You can't buy publicity like this. 'Producer of axe-murder telefilm found hacked to death!' It's the best thing that could have happened. Except for poor old Tip, of course. . . ."

So there it is, Lee thought. One minute everything is lost. The next minute . . .

"The trades will splash it all over the front page in the morning," Walter continued. "When they call, you have no statement, except for what a horrible, senseless act it was, blah blah. A couple of days from now, get ready for the interviews. I'll arrange everything. You'll be on *A Current Affair*, *E! Entertainment*. . . . Jenny, too, if she wants."

Lee raised his hand, holding Walter off. "That's enough. I don't like it. Jenny won't, either. There's a limit."

"How do you mean?"

"Have you ever lost anyone, Walter?"

"What kind of a question is that? You have my sympathy—absolutely. But now it's time to get with the program. Ride this out and you can parlay it into your own production company, first-run indie syndication, 'created by' credits . . ."

Lee walked on, leaving Walter alone and babbling to the trees that whipped violently now as the wind gained strength. A fogbank blew across the moon, masking its light. Somewhere a dog was barking, not blocks away this time, but nearby. The residents were not allowed pets. Paulino had said something about dogs finding a way into the grounds, going for the garbage. But tonight the garbage was already outside the fence.

Suddenly the barking changed into a yowl.

"What's the matter with that mutt?" said Walter, catching up.

"He's in pain," said Lee.

It was true. The yowl rose in pitch, then ceased abruptly, cut off. It was very close by.

On the other side of the trees, a door creaked open. Footsteps sharp as pistol shots ran down a suspended stairway.

Then there was a scream.

"What the hell . . . ?" Walter began.

A tree branch broke loose and sailed end-over-end into the lamppost they had just passed. The opaque fixture shattered with a pop and bits of curved glass, frosted white and thin as eggshells, fell around them on the stones. Walter ducked and covered his head, as the rest of the light fixtures on the path went out.

They must be wired in circuit, Lee thought, as they were plunged into darkness.

"Jesus Christ!" yelled Walter. "What . . . ?"

Lee heard someone crying, and left the path. "Over here. . . ."

Through the descending mist he saw the windows of the condos, and the vague, diffused movements of stick figures behind yellow blinds. Was what he had heard the soundtrack of a TV show?

Walter hobbled over, brushing off his expensive slacks. "Great. These are Italian wool."

"Shh."

The wind subsided and the crying became clearer. It was hard to make out but there seemed to be someone squatting down on the walkway in front of the next building, a grainy commotion of some sort in the thick shadows.

Was someone hurt?

As Lee approached, a face looked up at him and he realized that it was a child. The Becker boy, the fifth-grader Jenny had tutored in English last year.

"Philip?"

The face sharpened as the mist fell away and he saw the wide eyes and quivering chin.

"What's wrong, Philip?"

"It's Pokey!"

Lee had no idea who Pokey was, but he guessed that the Beckers had broken the rules by bringing an animal into their unit. They had certainly succeeded in keeping it out of sight until now.

"What happened?"

"Somebody hurted him!"

Mrs. Becker came down the stairs in a flowered housecoat, her arms out as if for balance.

"Philip! Are you all right?"

Lee knelt and reached with Philip to the shadowy mass on the sidewalk. He felt the dog's belly jerking, panting for air, then Philip's tiny hand moving against his, stroking the fur. The boy's fingers were wet.

"That *thing*! I told you not to feed him!" Mrs. Becker bent over the boy, grasping his shoulders roughly, dragging him to his feet. Philip resisted, crying louder.

"Does somebody have a flashlight?"

"Who's there?"

"It's Lee Marlow. Do you have—?"

"Joseph, come quick!"

Mr. Becker jiggled downstairs in his undershirt.

"Here. Use this." Walter flicked a slender, gold Dunhill lighter.

Lee took it and looked at the dog.

The animal lay on its side, in the middle of a dark spot. When Lee moved the lighter the spot remained; it was not a shadow. The boy combed his fingers through the black Labrador's short hair where it was matted around the collar. The hand came away covered with blood.

The boy wailed.

"Come!" said Mrs. Becker. She tried unsuccessfully to drag him away.

"Call a vet," said Lee.

"I'm not paying for no vet!" said Mr. Becker. "It ain't ours!"

Lee twisted the collar, looking for a tag, but there was none. Under the orange teardrop flame the dog's head lolled at an unnatural angle as he placed his fingers under the neck. The back of the neck opened like a pink mouth, revealing a cut that had almost severed the dog's head from its body.

"Forget the vet," Lee told them. "Take the boy inside."

The dog's sides spasmed, then did not move again.

Mr. Becker hauled off and struck the boy across the head. "I told you to leave that goddamn fleabag alone! Didn't I? *Didn't* I?"

"Now," Lee said.

"What are you doing?" said Walter.

Lee picked up the dog in his arms and carried it toward the apartment as the wind keened again through the trees. At the Beckers' door, he set the dog down on the welcome mat, under the porch light.

As Mrs. Becker hustled the boy indoors, Lee got a better look at the dog.

The cut was unmistakable. The animal had suffered a single powerful blow from something like a butcher's cleaver. Even the vertebrae at the top of the spinal column were chopped through; white gristle and spongy bone marrow shone under the oozing blood.

"Must've got in a dogfight," said Becker.

"The kind of animal that did that," Lee told him, "has two legs."

"No way! A coyote, maybe. . . ."

In the front room, Philip was inconsolable. Lee could not bring himself to look in at the boy, at the red, swimming eyes, the contorted mouth, the desolated posture as his mother dragged him by the armpits across the room.

For a chilling moment he felt the depth of the child's loss acutely, knew exactly what Philip was experiencing as he was locked in his room and inside himself. A great sadness hung in the air, rendering it heavy, like a thunderhead pendulant with tears and lightning in search of a target. A part of Lee wanted to get away, as far away as he could from the death he had carried in his arms, that now lay at his feet; but the stains on his hands and his clothes would remain, a mark that would not easily wash off.

He remembered the old saw about deaths in Hollywood always coming in threes. It was a superstition that seemed to run true to form, as if any death had an attraction for other deaths, a negative charge as real as static electricity. When a celebrity died, reporters watched like vultures for another and another to complete the pattern. . . . The greater truth, Lee now realized, was that death could be found everywhere. The pattern was not so simple, except to journalists who sought to complete it for the sake of a story. Each day many people in the industry went to their final rest, most of them not stars and so unnoticed; and beyond this town, in ever-widening circles, hundreds, thousands, millions more deaths in a wave that was unstoppable, each one merely a single point in a schematic too large and too inclusive to know or to bear.

The very earth itself was soaked in blood, and the stain would spread until it dissolved all boundaries. The attention paid to a specific passing, the sadness and regret, the grieving and consoling, was only a way of delaying a confrontation with the larger reality, substituting an illusion of manageability in the face of absolute powerlessness. It could not be put off forever. Death was the final purpose of everything that lives, the innermost essence of life itself.

Lee touched the dead dog one last time, measuring its dimensions in his hands, a body that had moved and would move no more, that had found its fulfillment and its destiny. He had not known the dog in life except for its howling at the moon from the next block, but he wanted to know it now in its truest, most natural state.

"*Oh* no, not inside! It's bleeding like a stuck pig. . . ."

Lee pitied Mr. Becker almost as much as he pitied the boy, who had never before looked death in the face and was at the beginning of a journey of understanding that would take a lifetime. He wiped his hands on his shirt and stood.

"May I use your phone?" he said.

"Who you gonna call now?" said Becker. "Animal Control?"

That's a good idea, thought Lee. "Yes," he said.

"Tell them to get this mess outta here! And tell 'em I ain't payin' for it! They can bill the owner, whoever *that* is. . . ."

"I will," said Lee. "But first, I want to talk to my wife."

To tell her not to be afraid, he thought, no matter what.

Jenny backed away from her front door.

She grappled blindly for the lamp and finally found it.

Libby stood there, her hair blowing wild.

"Are you all right, Jen?"

Jen. That was what Lee called her.

"I—I think so."

"Thank God. The way you sounded on the phone . . . I had second thoughts about leaving you alone. Look at you! You were sitting here in the dark, weren't you?"

149

"I'm okay." Jenny heard her own voice quavering, about to break. "Lee's still not here. It's been hours."

"Well, stop worrying," Libby said. "We'll get through this."

She heard the cool detachment in Libby's voice. Libby was always in control, her life and her emotions all neatly in place. Maybe it would help to have a friend here, after all.

And yet Jenny wondered about the anxiety in the pit of her stomach, why it was stronger now. The pain pills were beginning to work, but she felt nauseous.

"I just don't know," she said.

"I do."

"How?"

"Have the police contacted you?"

That was what Walter had asked. "Why should they?"

"Well, you were one of the last people to see him alive. Tipper or whatever his name is. Was. With the baseball cap."

"How do you know that?"

"They showed a picture of him on TV." Libby was restless. "How about a drink? You look like you need one."

"That bad, huh?"

"As a matter of fact, you look great. Like the woman in that movie. The fantasy. Uma something. She played Venus on the Half-Shell."

Jenny retied her robe self-consciously and

closed it at the throat. "Lee doesn't keep any liquor in the house."

"What a drag." Libby sloughed off her heavy coat and draped it over the end of the couch; without it she seemed much smaller, less formidable. "A real Type A personality."

"What's that?"

"The type that doesn't know how to relax. Workaholics. Sometimes they get heart attacks, if they're not careful."

"Lee's not a workaholic!"

"Whatever. Nothing personal."

The feeling was getting worse. It was more than the underlay of anxiety that was almost always with her, the perpetual edginess she had learned to live with. An awareness was dawning inside her. It had been a long time coming. There were still no words for the feeling, but now it was causing her heart to beat dangerously fast.

"There's nothing you can do here," she said. "Really."

"No?" Libby picked up the remote control and aimed it at the TV. "You know what I think? I think you need a friend tonight."

Onscreen, shadows gathered and took on color, sharpening into focus. It was another shot of the Home Show Channel building and the ramp to the underground garage.

"That's where Walter and I parked today," Jenny said. "It could have been either one of us."

"I don't think so."

"Why not?"

"You're too—lucky."

"I don't feel very lucky right now."

"You are. You have someone who watches over you, even when you don't know it."

"A Companion?" Now, at last, Jenny identified the source of the growing unease. "Libby, I want you to tell me again what Rose said."

"I told you, I don't recall her exact words."

Libby tapped the remote control, bringing the sound up in small steps until they could hear the reporter's words. The police had made no arrests yet and there were no clues, except that the victim was killed with a sharp, heavy instrument.

" 'The blade,' " Jenny said, remembering now. " 'The blade that falls.' Libby, what did that *mean*?"

"You'll have to ask Rose."

"I'm not asking Rose. I'm asking you. Why don't you want to talk about it? You're my friend, aren't you?"

"You know that. But Rose is the channel."

"Then call her." The phone was no longer on the table. She ran to the kitchen, snatched it from the wall and returned. She stood in front of the couch and held it out, moving the switch to ON.

"What . . . ?"

"I want to know!"

"You don't need that. Rose is already here."

Jenny backed away, the red LED on the handset glowing like a warning light.

"She'll always be with you now," Libby said. "We all will. The Sisters are here to help."

Jenny did not like the sound of that. "What are you saying?"

"I told you, I don't understand it, either. But—"

"Don't you? Libby, what do you know about what happened today?"

"I was with you, remember? Jenny, who am I?"

Jenny met her eyes. They were turned up at the corners, perpetually amused, the eyes of one who refused to take life too seriously, the perfect balance for Jenny's own insecurities. This was the same person who had helped her through the rough spots, after Rob left and later, when she met Lee and thought she was falling in love and was terrified. It was Libby who had stayed on the phone with her for hours night after night, seeing her through it, the one who was always there for her. Husbands and lovers had come and gone, but her friend remained.

"You're my friend," said Jenny.

"That's right. And I can see that you need to get out of here. You're starting to *fester*, Jenny. This whole house is. I can smell it. Your life here, and all that goes with it. Your mind is caught in a tape-loop. You've got to break the sequence."

"I can't. I have to wait for Lee."

"I'll bet you haven't eaten since this afternoon."

"I'm not hungry."

"Because you're trapped here in Misery Central! Look, tomorrow you're going to have to deal with reporters, the whole bit. The police, too— maybe tonight. You don't want to be here for that, do you?"

"I have to be here for Lee."

"Well, he's not here, is he?" Libby grabbed her coat. "Get dressed. We'll split a Chinese chicken salad at Hampton's."

"Well . . ."

"Then at least take a walk with me. Anything, before it's too late. Come on."

Jenny went upstairs as if sleepwalking, as if she no longer had a will of her own. It was easier this way. She was definitely not accomplishing anything by staying here. She pulled on a sweater, jeans and socks and toed into her tennis shoes.

As they left, Jenny felt a combination of guilt and release. Just for a while, she thought. That's all right, isn't it? I guess I have to eat. Even if I'm not hungry. . . .

On the sidewalk, she heard a chirping ring from inside the house.

"The phone," she said, starting back.

"What phone? I don't hear anything."

"It could be Lee. . . ."

Libby caught her elbow and led her away, as if she were a child.

"It's the wind."

"Are you sure?"

"Listen."

It swished in the trees and whistled down the buildings, moaning in the hollows of stairwells and doorways, rattling screens and stirring leaves into a frenzy.

"Let's get gone," Libby said. "This place gives me the creeps."

154

Chapter 11

Lee let the phone ring ten times before he put it down.

"Well?" said Walter.

"She's still not home." Even the answering machine is off, he thought.

He replaced the Beckers' phone on the dining room table, next to a bowlful of walnuts that had been dipped in gold paint. Against one wall, an armoire displayed a set of limited-edition collectors' plates honoring various film stars, including Marilyn Monroe, John Wayne, Clark Gable,

Dennis Etchison

Shirley Temple and a dozen more in their most famous roles. Lee identified the faces of Klaus Kinski and Hanna Schygulla, but on closer examination saw that they were only Woody Allen and Madonna.

In another room, Philip wailed uncontrollably. Lee heard the mother's voice pleading and then a slap. The boy wailed louder. The door to the dining room burst open and Mr. Becker lumbered out, breathing heavily.

"Did you call?" he said.

"I couldn't get through."

"Jesus, what am *I* supposed to do with it?" He yelled for his wife. "Minda!"

"I'll take care of it," said Lee. Then, to Walter: "Give me your coat."

"What for?"

"I want to cover it."

Walter followed Lee's gaze through the living room to the porch, where the dog's remains lay in a glossy mound on the mat. "Not this jacket. It's a Versace!"

Lee crossed the living room and opened the screen door. He leaned down and got his fingers under the sides of the welcome mat and prepared to lift the dog on it.

Mrs. Becker was behind him, holding out a plastic garbage bag.

"You can put it in this."

"Take it down and dump it in the trash!" shouted her husband. "I don't care, just get the damn thing out of here!"

Lee opened the plastic bag and slipped it around the mat.

"It smells," said Mrs. Becker.

"Don't worry," said Lee. "I'll get rid of it." He stood, twisting the bag shut and lifting the contents off the porch.

"What about the blood?" she said.

Lee started down the stairs. "Try hosing it off."

Walter followed him down. "Nice. Now what are we supposed to do?"

I can't leave it on their porch, thought Lee. If I put it downstairs, other animals may come, attracted by the scent; he pictured teeth tearing the plastic to get at the carrion inside. And I can't just toss it in the Dumpster. It's not a piece of garbage.

"I'll keep it till Animal Control gets here."

"That might not be tonight."

"Go home, Walter," Lee said. "You've done your part."

Walter did not resist the suggestion.

"Well, remember what I said about the press. . . ."

"I'll refer all calls to you. And Walter? Forget the interviews. Make whatever statement you want, but Jenny and I don't want to talk to any reporters. If the police get in touch . . ."

"Call Mark at Kalisch and Fischer. You have the number?"

"Yeah. Now you better get going. You can find your way, can't you?"

"Right. I'm out of here."

Lee looked back in the direction of the pool

and the rec room. All the lights were still on except for the lampposts along the tree-lined path, leaving a wall of blackness between here and the front gate.

"That way, right?"

"Right. Past the trees, then straight ahead."

"Gotcha. If you need anything—"

"Don't call us. I'll call you."

Lee watched him pass between the waving trees as another gust of wind snaked through the grounds, disrupting everything in its wake, like an invisible presence speeding relentlessly toward some unseen purpose. Walter paused long enough to turn and shout:

"Tell Jenny she did great!"

Then he was gone into the darkness.

Lee cut between the buildings, avoiding the unlighted path. Cradling the heavy plastic bag, he thought, Someone is going to miss this dog. Someone on the next block or the next, who will call for their pet but Spot or Rover or Towser will not be home tonight. He imagined himself leaving the complex and walking the streets with the package in his arms, listening for a whistle or a voice that shouted *Here, boy!* as he watched every porch for an untouched bowl of kibble, a forlorn face at a window, a lonely child standing watch as the wind taunted and mocked, testing screen doors and scattering raked leaves and howling down the empty streets, going away.

Who would do a thing like this? The dog had been struck by a large blade, with nearly enough force to cut the head off. And Lee had almost been there in time to see it. . . .

Some chickenshit teenager? A gang kid with a machete? A tough guy who drives heavy machinery by day and keeps a hatchet by the back door, a psycho Vietnam vet who sleeps with a bayonet under his pillow? Not an animal, no, but a human being who acts on his angers without concern for the consequences, for what it might do to someone else. That's evil, he thought. Someone without conscience is someone less than fully human.

He passed glowing windows behind which people sat watching television, as if the windows themselves were television screens, the buildings nothing more than false fronts on some backlot, a set inhabited by extras waiting for the director to return and tell them what to do. And behind one of those windows, lurking in a doorway or hiding in the bushes, was the one who had done this thing, who had slaughtered a living being for no reason.

"Hey!" he shouted. "Why don't you come on out?"

The only answer was the wind at his back, a sound deceptively like whimpering.

"Here, this is what you wanted! Come and get it!"

The whimpering continued. It was a human voice, after all. He turned in time to see a short figure duck out of sight in the bushes.

"You! Did you do this?"

The figure showed itself.

It was Philip.

Lee gave a nod. The boy came running and caught up with him. They walked on together.

"Where are you going?" said the boy.

"Home," said Lee.

"Is it far?"

"Just on the other side of those buildings."

The boy wiped his nose on his sleeve. "Was he your doggie?"

"No. Do you know where he lived?"

"He always came over after school. I gave him lots of stuff. Hot dogs. Cheese. He liked cheese."

"Did he?"

"Yeah. He was a good dog."

"I'll bet he was."

They kept walking, farther away from the path now, through the grass. Lee could not see his own house yet.

"Are you gonna bury him?"

"Do you think I should?" Lee asked.

The boy nodded solemnly.

It seemed like a good idea. The Animal Control truck would simply dispose of it like so much spoiled meat. Even a dog deserved better than that. He decided that he might not call them at all.

"Where?" Lee asked. "We need a good place."

"Um, a tree."

"Which one?"

The boy shrugged.

"We'll do it in the morning, then."

As soon as he said it, however, Lee thought again of the wandering packs of wild dogs, coyotes and raccoons that might be drawn to it out in the open before morning. On the other hand, did he really want to keep it till then? Where would he put it?

He would have a hard enough time explaining to Jenny about the blood on his clothes.

"My dad won't let me," said the boy. "But I can get up real early. . . ."

"Does your dad know where you are now?"

"I sneaked out. Through the window."

"Don't you think you'd better tell him, and your mom, so they don't worry?"

"No."

Neither do I, thought Lee.

"Where's your shovel?" said the boy.

Lee heard the wind playing tricks again. It sounded like people talking over by the path, though it could have come from any direction. The buildings served as baffles, deflecting the sound waves in unexpected ways, magnifying the falling of leaves on cement so that they could be footsteps, the wind the chattering of human voices.

"I'll see if I have one," said Lee.

If I don't, he thought, I'll dig the grave with my bare hands. Whatever it takes to do it right.

In other clothes Walter would have been a different man.

For example, with jeans, sneakers and a shorter haircut, one that lay in a more casual fashion over his forehead, would come a more relaxed gait and an easier smile, though the emphasis would then be on his long, dour face. In a three-piece suit he would seem older and more uptight, the wiry hair brushed closer to his head, calling even greater attention to his pallor.

Only in bathing trunks would he look to be exactly what he was, a middle-aged man beginning to go soft around the middle and loose in the arms, with graying chest hair that belied the dyed strands he usually combed across the top of his head. As it was, in pleated wool trousers to suggest a strength to his legs that was no longer there and a full-cut sport shirt to hide the fleshiness, the oversized jacket to add heft to his arms and shoulders and the curled hair at the back of his bulldog neck, he fit his part perfectly.

The look included thin-soled loafers and narrow belts incapable of holding the hi-rise slacks above his hips, and required that he walk with slower, more measured steps, pausing routinely every few seconds to touch his shirt at the waist to be sure it was tucked in and his gut properly concealed. The overall effect was of a man who had made a premature jump in social class a few years ago, long enough to forget his origins but not long enough to feel at ease in a town where appearances were everything and details were scrutinized from blocks away, a town of dreams bought and sold, dominated by actors and agents, where people dreamed of living in dream houses and life itself was a dream, a fantasy performed in an arranged setting under a perpetually flattering sun, instead of the hard reality it was for those who lived elsewhere.

Walter kept moving, regardless. The operant principle for his life was that a moving target is harder to identify, responsibility less likely to adhere to someone not locked into a continuing role, a character at once on the make for a better part and his own pimp, whose obituary would list gross profit participation and onscreen credits as the only statistics worth mentioning.

He had just passed the pool, on his way to the front gate, when he heard the voices.

He did not stop, did not even pause. From the studio apartments on the other side of the dwarf palm trees came the sound of newscasts, all reporting the same story, of the murder this afternoon in Beverly Hills. As if reluctant to be identified as one of the minor players in this sensational melodrama, he lowered his chin and stared down at the path as he emerged from the darkness.

Now there were colored circles on the ground ahead, from spotlights on the roof of the recreation room. The wind came up again and a white plastic chair toppled into the pool with a splash, floating briefly and knocking against the concrete lip before sinking below the surface. Trees waved rubbery leaves in the overcast sky and the fronds of the tropical shrubbery undulated near the wrought-iron enclosure. Within the rec room, a green Ping-Pong table had the polished sheen of a worn craps table under a single hooded bulb. Walter turned up his collar and pressed on toward the gate, his fists in his jacket pockets.

The gate was a tall frame with welded iron bars and a solid square of reinforced steel to protect the electronically activated latch. Outside the gate were the residents' mailboxes, locked panels bolted to a stucco wall, and a sidewalk leading across the lawn to the street. In the street, every parking space was taken, the cars nearest the entrance awash with colorful reflections from the spotlights in front of the complex. The tops of the cars squirmed with shadows as tree branches overhead jerked and trembled in the rising wind. Crisp leaves blew against the tires and collected in the gutters, as the Santa Ana shrieked around rearview mirrors and whistled through the gate, groaning in the open-air foyer as if it were a wind tunnel.

Walter removed one hand from his jacket and grasped the latch.

"Help me . . ." said a voice.

He let go of the handle as if jolted by a charge of static electricity.

There was no one behind him.

"Over here," said the voice, "please . . . !"

Where?

"Please!"

The voice came from the end of the short tunnel, and somewhere to the right, where the doorway to the rec room stood open.

"Can I help you?" Walter said.

There was a figure just inside, half-hidden by the edge of the door.

"Excuse me, but I'm trying to find someone. There are no names on the mailboxes. . . ."

"I wouldn't know," said Walter. "I don't live here."

"Haven't you heard of the Marlows?"

Beyond the door, the lightbulb swung back and

164

forth, causing the shadows under the green table to lengthen against a pile of towels on the floor. The rasping voice sounded like a woman, though it had a confusingly androgynous quality. The face remained bisected. The half that he could see had no distinct features. Was that because of the backlight?

"Twenty-three nineteen," Walter said. "But they're not home."

"Oh, I see. I'll wait, then."

"Lee's already here, but he's not in the house yet. Give him a few more minutes." Walter gestured at the simulated forest that was the grounds. "Go down the path . . ."

"It's so dark."

"Wait here, then. Jenny should be home soon. If she doesn't park in the garage, in which case—"

"You know Jennifer?"

"She's my client."

"Then you must be . . ."

"Walter Heim. Creative Artists International. And you're . . . ?"

Passing the pool enclosure, Jenny spotted something white floating under the water.

Was it only the moon's reflection? She could not be sure, the way the wind whipped the surface. She paused by the railing for a better look.

Overhead, the sky was milky with the moon barely showing through the mist. And there below was its glowing circle, pale and hyaline, rocking on the wavelets in the deep end.

Another whiteness, however, lay in the shallow end nearest her. It seemed to have arms and legs. She rubbed her elbows, chilled, and backed away from the iron rail.

Where was Libby?

I shouldn't have let her go ahead for the car, she thought.

Jenny knew the way to the front gate well enough. But tonight something was wrong. The last days and hours seemed to be building a momentum that would require some sort of terrible climax. So many details, meaningless in themselves, now attached to the deaths of Lee's parents, Tip's murder this afternoon and Lee's absence tonight, lending each event new weight. It was impossible for her to know where it was leading, but she had a strong sense that whatever the process was it could not be diverted. She could not simply step aside and let it pass her by, for she was a part of it.

Just let me make it through the night, she thought. This night. And then maybe, just maybe, things will snap back in the morning. . . .

Lee, I need you!

At least she had Libby.

Or did she?

It was getting darker. There were no lights on the path. Whenever there had been a power failure before, it had not lasted for long. Someone from Maintenance & Security would show up and chuck the right switch, change the fuse or whatever it was they did, and order would be restored in a matter of minutes. Where were they now? Paulino was probably home in bed, but someone was on call, weren't they? She glanced back at the way she had come. The tall trees formed a wall of impenetrable blackness, as if to discourage her from returning to her house.

She knew now why she had paused by the pool enclosure in the first place. It was because of the sounds. The way the wind resonated in the drainpipes and rattled the screen doors and set the lampposts to creaking, and the splashing of water and the clanging of the front gate ahead, as though someone were shaking it like the bars of a cage.

Wasn't Libby outside already?

"Over here," said a voice.

Where was it coming from?

"Here!"

With the wind singing in her ears, she could not be sure.

Then she saw someone on the flagstone path, coming this way.

"Libby . . . ?"

"Well, who do you think?"

It was her friend's voice and her face above the collar of the heavy coat. Hearing her words, Jenny left the iron fence. Now she saw the plastic chairs around the pool, some of them tipped over by the wind, and realized that the whiteness below the surface was one of these chairs, lying upside down so that its arms and legs pointed at the moon. With Libby here again, details receded into a more normal perspective, unremarked aspects of a familiar landscape.

"Did you get the car?"

"Not yet."

"You know, you don't have to park on the street. Next time use the garage. I'll give you the code. . . ."

"I can't get out," said Libby. "The gate won't open."

"Sure it will. All you do is turn the handle. It's not locked from the inside."

"See for yourself."

Their footsteps rang as they walked the last few yards through the short tunnel.

"Here," said Libby. "You try it."

Jenny grasped the latch. It turned, but only an inch, no more. Libby was right. It was jammed.

"Oh, for God's sake. What is *wrong* with this thing . . . ?"

Then she noticed the marks. Something had struck the steel reinforcement over the lock, chipping the paint so that bare metal showed through. The plate was knocked out of alignment, just enough to prevent the mechanism from clearing the frame.

"It looks like someone tried to break in," Jenny said, incredulous.

"Did they?"

"Look at the marks. Like they hit it with a . . . what do you call it? Sledgehammer. At least they didn't get in. . . ."

"Not in," said Libby. "The marks are on this side. Somebody was trying to break *out*."

"Why? Why would they? It always opens from inside."

"Then they wanted to wreck it, so it wouldn't."

Not a sledgehammer, thought Jenny. The gouges were sharp and narrow, in a single downward line.

"I'll call Security."

"How are you going to do that?" said Libby.

"Over here. There's a phone."

Jenny led her out of the foyer to the rec room.

The door was open. Inside, a Ping-Pong table, three smaller tables with chairs, soda and food machines, a bulletin board, an inflatable air mattress for the pool and a white flotation ring with rope attached, and a pile of used towels. The wind followed them in, causing the hooded bulb to swing slowly, casting shadows that expanded and contracted.

Jenny went to the phone. "Do you have any change? I forgot my purse."

Libby took a wallet out of her coat pocket and unsnapped the coin compartment. "Just pennies and nickels."

"It takes dimes and quarters."

"Here." Libby handed over a dollar bill. "Buy a Coke and get change."

Jenny smoothed the dollar, unfolding the corners, and inserted it into the drink machine. It immediately rolled out of the slot, rejected. She flattened it and tried again, but the bill was too soft and full of wrinkles.

"Give me another one."

"Let's see. A ten, two twenties . . . Nope. That's the only single I've got."

"Great." Jenny leaned against the Coke machine, momentarily defeated.

"Forget Security. How do we get out?"

"We have to walk all the way back. There's a service entrance on the west side. Or we could go through the parking garage."

"Where's that?"

"Not as far." She had a mental image of Tip in another garage, on his knees in his stupidly trendy clothes, pleading before someone took his life. She could not come up with a picture of the killer beyond a tall, bulky figure with something in its hand. . . . "But I—I really don't want to go down there. Not tonight."

Libby understood. "All right, we go back."

Jenny did not like the idea of walking all that way again, even with someone. Was there an alternative?

"We could wait here, till somebody comes in. When they open the gate . . ."

"It won't open. It's jammed."

Libby was right.

"This is like one of those dreams," Jenny said, "when you're running and you can't get anywhere. You know, the monster's chasing you but you can't get away?"

"Dream, my ass," said Libby. "This is ridiculous. Give me that dollar. I'm going to knock on the first door I see and get some change. I don't intend to stand here all night!"

Outside, there was a crash.

Jenny looked through the plate glass window, through the ghostly image of herself and Libby under the swaying light fixture, and saw a small, round object the size of a human head roll to a stop inside the pool enclosure. It was the top of one of the tiki lamps, black and sooty, with a pale wick sticking out of the top. At least it was not lit.

"What's *happening* to this place?" said Libby.

"The wind."

"So?"

"They call it a Santa Ana. It comes up from the Gulf of Mexico. . . ."

"No way," said Libby. "Santa Anas are warm. This one acts like some kind of tropical storm. What did they say on the news?"

"I don't know. I never got to the weather report."

"Hurricane Lizzie."

"That," said Jenny, "is not very funny."

Now the wind picked up visible speed, as the palm trees bent over like catapults about to launch their razor-sharp fronds. They watched in disbelief as the surface of the pool churned into whitecaps and the rest of the plastic chairs skittered forward. What was next? A waterspout?

Jenny left the window to close the door. Then she returned to stand with Libby as a powerful gust of wind hit the glass full-on. The pane bowed, distorting the reflection of the two women, the green table and the pile of used towels breathing behind them.

"It's going to break, isn't it?" said Libby. "You know what? You're right. This *is* a nightmare."

The foliage twisted and re-formed, as if the world within the complex was not, had not ever been secure, the surroundings malleable and subject to any manner of change, like the props of a film set waiting to be struck and rebuilt into endlessly new patterns. Jenny searched her memory for the missing details that might bring it all together, in a pattern that had some meaning.

"Hurricane Rose," she said slowly.

Libby laughed. "I like that better. You know, there's no need to be afraid of her. Rose wouldn't do anything to harm you, I promise. We're here to help."

"Why won't you tell me what kind of help?"

"Whatever you need—that's our task. Or rather the Companions. They watch out for the living."

"What was it she said?"

"We already had this conversation, didn't we? Blades. Blades that fall. Remember?"

"Not that part. Before."

Jenny was thinking about the murder this afternoon, the way it had happened. For some reason she had a flash of Andrew Borden in 1892, how he had been found in his sitting room with his head cleaved open and his face practically sliced off, one eye hanging down his cheek . . .

" 'The Companions are two,' wasn't it?"

" 'Two sisters . . .' " said Libby.

" 'One serves the light . . . and one the darkness,' " Jenny finished for her.

Now she thought of the gate outside. The vertical cuts on the lockplate, as if something heavy had come down on it, swung full-force. Something like—

"And the light," Libby said, stepping away from the window.

Jenny watched her reflection, the hooded bulb overhead, tilting like a Chinese peasant's hat, the light swaying on its cord so that Libby's face was divided, one half in darkness for seconds at a time.

" 'Don't turn away from the light . . .' " Libby said. "Oh!"

Libby backed past the end of the table, slipped and fell. She went down fast, disappearing from sight as if something had yanked her off her feet.

Jenny turned from the window.

The other woman had fallen into the pile of dirty towels.

"Are you hurt?"

"Christ, no." Libby tried to get up. "I just slipped on something, that's all. . . ."

There was a wet spot on the floor. The used towels were still damp and some of the pool water had leaked out of them and formed a puddle. As Libby pushed against the towels, more water squeezed out.

"They shouldn't leave these here," Libby said. "I could have broken something and filed an insurance claim! You know, a neck brace, the whole bit. I could . . ."

"The laundry service is supposed to pick them up." Every Tuesday and Friday, Jenny thought, along with a bundle of clean ones. They must have skipped a day. The pile was large, two or three feet tall. And still wet. A lot of people must have gone in the pool today. She had not seen any, though. Who would go swimming in weather like this? And the shelf of new towels was practically empty. It was as if someone had pulled them all down onto the floor. . . .

Libby held out her hand and Jenny gave her a tug to set her on her feet. Jenny's hand was wet.

"Oops," Libby said. "Sorry. I need a dry one." She picked up a towel from the pile, then another.

Jenny stared at her own hand. It was wet, too. It was also dark, like the stain on the cement floor, the stain that was growing as more dark fluid squeezed out of the pile.

She lifted the next towel and they both saw that those farther down were even darker.

"They're all so dirty. . . ." Libby said.

Then she let go and put her hands to her mouth.

Staring up at them from deep within the pile was the blood-spattered face of the late Walter Heim.

Chapter 12

Lee carried the bag toward the houses on the west side. The wind was fierce now. He and the boy had to fight it every step of the way.

They found an acacia tree that was not specifically a part of anyone's property but belonged to the development. He decided he had a right. It was what his usage fees had been for all this time. If the Homeowners' Association wanted to make something of it, let them.

"I'll get something to dig with," Lee said. He

put the dog down under the tree. "You wait here."

"Can I go with you?"

"You better watch him. I'll be right back."

"Okay," the boy said uncertainly.

Lee climbed a low hillock and finally saw his own house, the patio, the narrow backyard ending at the security wall. I don't have a shovel, he thought, only some small hand tools. I need something that will go deep. . . .

As he came around the side of the house, he noticed that the living room lamp was on.

Jenny had not answered his buzz from the gate, or the phone. Was she home now?

He sidestepped the flower bed and came to the front door.

"Jen?"

When there was no answer, he took out his keys.

In the living room, the high-intensity lamp cast an inverted triangle of white light against the ceiling. The imprint of her body was still in the cushions of the sofa.

"Jenny, are you here?"

Though the walls diffused the light some shadows remained in the dark mouth of the fireplace, the pleats of the curtains, the hallway to the kitchen and at the top of the stairs.

Was she asleep?

As he mounted the stairs, he heard a scratching from the bedroom.

The bathroom light was on, cutting a severe geometry across the floor and the foot of the bed.

The sheets and blankets lay in twisted folds that might have been a human form.

The scratching grew louder, more insistent.

He started across the room.

It was only a branch outside the window. The form in the bed was a pillow half-covered by the sheet. He pressed his hand on the mattress and felt that it was cold. The branch tapped, moving against the pane like a finger with a broken nail swiping at a blackboard. Below, the grounds appeared deserted. He could not see the place where he had left the boy, but he wanted to return to the grave site as soon as possible and finish it.

The bathroom was cold but humid, with snail tracks left by moisture that had condensed and dripped down the mirror and the walls. The drops resembled marks that might spell out a message on the glass, one that could only be read when the bathroom filled with steam again. He touched the switch plate to cut off the light and went downstairs, a wet residue on his fingertips.

Her purse was on the table in front of the sofa, next to the telephone handset.

She wouldn't leave without her purse, he thought. Not unless she was in a big hurry.

He had no time to solve the mystery now. He would be back in a few minutes. Then he would sort it out. . . .

He entered the short hall, on his way to the kitchen. What tools did he have in the yard? He remembered a trowel. It would have to do.

The door to the guest room was closed and the

downstairs bathroom was dark and empty. He went through to the kitchen, and heard someone clear her throat.

"Jenny?"

A rasping, somewhere across the dark kitchen.

He saw the gleaming contours of the stove and refrigerator, the polished grain of the cabinets, the vinyl covering on the chairs around the breakfast table. A band of light wavered over the window as a car drove by on the street, the headlights spilling over the top of the security wall and into the backyard. Then there was only a tiny red glow, like the eye of a small animal that had crawled halfway up the tiles by the sink.

The rasping sound came again.

He realized that it was from the two-way intercom in the telephone's base unit, as the cordless receiver picked up stray signals in the neighborhood. The red light indicated that the handset was not in its cradle. That was right; it was in the living room, where she had left it.

A second red light came into view by the sink. That would be the answering machine on the counter. It meant that there were messages on the tape, waiting to be replayed.

He had heard the rasping before, whenever a police car went by outside or a neighbor's phone locked onto the same frequency. Did that mean others heard squeals and phantom rings from his phone, as well?

He took the flashlight from the drawer and went out to the yard.

He found a rake, a hoe, pruning clippers and a trowel, but nothing stronger. Just as he had thought. He took the trowel and started out of the yard.

And stopped.

Someone was watching him.

Who?

He was sure of it. It was the old feeling that *something* was studying him from close range, biding its time.

Was Jenny in the house, after all?

It was impossible. He had checked all the rooms. He could believe his own eyes, couldn't he?

The house was empty.

He saw nothing in the yard that should not have been there. A patch of grass, the gate to the patio, the flower beds where the new tomatoes drooped amid fluttering leaves torn by the wind, and the tiny clusters of embryonic vegetables ready to drop into the mulch. Another car passed outside the grounds and the wind blew over the wall with a mournful lowing.

He thought of the boy waiting with the dog back under the tree, not more than a few hundred yards from here. Waiting for him to return.

I'm coming, he thought.

Where would he get a shovel? He could go to the next house or one of the condos, knock on doors with a lame excuse until he found what he needed and talk them into borrowing it. What time was it? He had lost track of the hour. He tried to read his watch but could not make it out.

Then he remembered Paulino.

The gardener had been carrying a shovel. The toolshed was down by the service gate, at the end of a maintenance path that cut diagonally across the grounds from the main entrance and the rec room. The service gate, the Dumpsters and Paulino's shed were almost adjacent to his property.

The wind pummeled his ears with Philip's voice.

Hurry!

It won't be long now, he thought.

The shed was padlocked. There was some equipment set out on one side: a metal canister for spraying insecticide, a gallon of plant nutrient, a pair of rubber gloves, a bundle of redwood stakes and a carton of jars and coffee cans that contained galvanized nails. In the beam of the security floodlight they looked like porcupine quills.

He used his flashlight to check the other side of the shed.

There was a long wooden handle. What was at the end? He lifted it and was surprised at its weight. A steel clamshell of some sort.

He remembered seeing it in Paulino's hands one day, over by the fence that separated the studio apartments from the condos. He had used it to sink a four-by-four into a hole filled with freshly poured cement. A post-hole digger, was that what it was called?

It would do.

He propped it on his shoulder and headed back.

The wind was constant now, sweeping through the open grassy areas, whipping the shrubbery and pounding the trees. Lee's face was numb, as though the nerves in his skin were shutting down, no longer responsive to the relentless battering. His mind, however, remained more sensitive than ever to the overpowering feeling that someone was following him.

It had started in the house.

What did it mean? As a child he had believed that the feeling was a warning not to open the closet or look under the bed. He had heeded it, and eventually the sense of danger left him. It was no more real now than it had been then. To believe otherwise meant that there had always been something in his room, waiting to get him, despite the fact that the closet was always empty come morning and only dust devils were under the bed.

Why had the feeling returned now?

It had to do with all that had happened. First his parents' accident. No, not an accident—someone actually tried to kill them, and succeeded. Paranoia? He had the evidence. And then the murder this afternoon, if Walter was telling the truth. And Walter never lied; that required imagination.

What did the three deaths have in common? Absolutely nothing. Except that all affected his life dramatically. Beyond that there could be no meaning, unless he inferred that their deaths occurred *because* of their connection to him, as if he were the focus of a vast and subtle plot. That way lay madness.

The only connection was the thread that binds everything together. The interlocking nature of the universe, the interrelationship of all things, as quantum physics suggested. That did not mean he was a spider at the center of a web that extended throughout the cosmos. To make that jump would mean that he really was paranoid, a psychic casualty stopped dead in his tracks by the discovery of coincidence.

Still, he had the feeling more intensely now than ever before.

Was his unconscious trying to tell him something? An inescapable conclusion that had already been drawn by the pattern-making part of his mind, the sum total of all the unnoticed details and unfinished thoughts of the last few days and hours? Or was he losing it, on his way to full-blown psychosis?

He tried to remain rational. If someone wanted to do him harm, they had failed. Killing Tip had not stopped the project from going ahead. Ironically, it now ensured that *Liz* would reach the tube, after all.

First his parents.

Then the man who was to be his producer or something like it, though they had never met.

Who's next?

My agent?

My wife?

I should have called Libby's, to see if Jenny's there.

I'll do it in a few minutes, he thought. As soon as I take care of the boy.

He hurried on through the grass, the wind pressing at his back like a force tracking his every move.

That's crazy, he thought.

But the feeling did not go away.

Philip did not open the bag. He remained hunkered down on the grass with his arms around his knees. The windows of the distant condos were yellow eyes winking through the waving leaves and branches. The moon tinged the grass with a wan glow, each drop of moisture that clung to the blades magnifying a tiny portion of the light like miniature lenses trembling as the wind passed over.

For a moment the wind subsided.

The droplets, however, continued to tremble, inches above the earth.

Someone was approaching.

Then a silhouette towered over him, holding something long and heavy.

"This will work," Lee said.

"Can I help?"

"I'll do it." Lee brought the post-hole digger down. There was a crunching as a divot of grass tore loose.

The boy scuttled aside and watched.

Lee lifted the tool and let its point drop again. He worked up a rhythm, lifting and dropping.

"It doesn't have to be too deep for now," he said. "I can help."

"No, that's all right." Holding the tool for another drop, he reconsidered. "Unless you want to. I guess he was sort of your dog."

"Yeah."

"Here. You can move the dirt. Just watch out for your hands."

"Okay."

The boy scooped the damp loam as best he could, cupping his miniature hands together. Somewhere an electrical wire buzzed, crackling whenever the wind gained force.

"I want you to remember him," Lee said. "This dog—you loved him, and he loved you. When you think of him, make it the good times. The way you played together. He was always there for you, whenever you needed him."

"Sometimes he wouldn't come."

"Then think of all the times he was there, and how much fun you had. Not the way he is now."

The boy cried softly, scooping the earth away. The hole was rough, chopped out in a shape that was not circular, the best Lee could do with no light but the moon. Soon it would be deep enough. The dirt broke apart and worms glistened and flexed in the boy's hands. A look of horror crossed his upturned face.

"Are they going to eat him?"

Lee did not answer. He kept digging. Finally he said, "We'll tie the bag shut. Real tight. So they can't get in."

Philip crawled on his knees to the bag.

"Don't," said Lee. "Don't look inside."

The boy waited, as Lee chopped deeper.

"It's deep enough," said the boy.

"No, it's not." Lee continued to pound away, cutting into adobe and rock. "Just a little bit more. . . ."

The boy looked around nervously.

"What is it?" Lee said.

"Somebody's coming."

The only sound Lee heard was the pounding of the heavy tool's blades, and the wind as it moved with seeming randomness through the grounds, striking unpredictably at window screens and the benches along the path beyond the big trees, whining through the plastic chairs by the pool, teasing and splashing the surface of the water.

"Your father?"

"I don't think so. Hey, mister, when are you gonna be finished?"

"Soon."

The blades struck the hard, woody roots of the acacia tree. Lee raised and dropped the digger again and again, unwilling to give up, hammering with greater force, chipping away with each blow.

"You better stop now."

"Get away!"

"But *mister* . . . !"

The digger would not go any deeper. The roots were too thick. Lee came to his senses and stopped himself.

"Lee," he said, leaning on the handle and

catching his breath. "Not mister. My name's Lee. Everybody has a name. What did you call your dog?"

"Pokey."

"That's right. I remember."

He dropped the tool and tied a double knot at the end of the bag, pulling it so tight that the plastic nearly tore. Then he lifted the bag gently and set it into the hole.

"Say something to Pokey. Tell him you love him. Go ahead. You won't have another chance. If you don't tell him now, he'll never know."

The little boy peered down into the hole. "Pokey . . ."

Then he looked up.

The sound of Lee's digging had not stopped. It echoed back and forth between the buildings, a dull, throbbing heartbeat. The dirt beside the hole crumbled in response to the rhythm.

The boy's eyes opened wide.

The wind blew harder, masking the sound, ripping a path through the darkness. It had begun somewhere back by the Dumpsters and Lee's house, moving relentlessly this way. The wind paused for a second as if inhaling, sucking in the power of the night. Lee heard the moist crunching, closer than ever. It was the sound of footsteps, very heavy, almost upon them.

Before Philip could speak, the wind tore the words away from his open mouth.

"What is it?" Lee said. "Can you hear me? I said—"

He saw Philip's eyes again, and glanced over his shoulder.

So this is how it happens, he thought calmly. So many years, all leading to this moment. This is what it was about. It was there, it always was, after all, and it still is. It has finally chosen to reveal itself. It's here now.

A dark figure stood behind him. As he turned to face it the figure raised its arms, lifting a long, heavy handle in its hands. It held that position for a beat, silhouetted against the moon. Something glinted at the end of the handle. Then the arms swung down in a swift, black blur, as all the lights in the complex went out.

Chapter 13

The lightbulb in the rec room went off.

Jenny was ready to run as soon as she saw Walter's bloody face. Now she had to get out. Beyond the window, as far as she could see, the entire complex had suffered a massive power failure. Trees and buildings were no longer distinguishable; only the pool stirred with a faintly reflective luminescence, like the writhing torso of a humpbacked whale.

Her impulse was still to dash for the door, but she did not want to bump into something and fall, as Libby had. The soles of her shoes squeaked on the wet floor.

"Where are you?" called Libby.

"This way!"

"Which way is that?"

"Here!"

Jenny rushed the door, the sticky floor sucking at her feet.

"Hold on!" said Libby. "I can't see . . . !"

Jenny stumbled out into the dark wind. Somewhere a power line sizzled. The wind struck her in the face with shocking force, as if someone had slapped her. Now it boxed her ears, garbling Libby's words. She broke from the rec room and entered the covered archway, where the wind howled like a runaway train in a blind tunnel.

A few steps more and she was in the open again.

Libby tried to catch up. "Wait . . . !"

"Follow me!"

There was another path, Jenny remembered. Paulino's shortcut across the grounds, to the western boundary.

Tall trees swayed, black clusters animated against an even greater darkness. The buildings were shadowed cliffs, towering ominously, with no lights in any windows. Jenny saw the moon overhead, above clawed branches that scratched the sky to reveal a few scattered stars. She felt grass beneath her shoes, and finally the worn dirt of the secret path. She forced herself to follow it, placing one foot heel-to-toe in front of the other.

Her eyes burned, as though the wind were

removing a layer of skin from her pupils. As her eyes opened wider she was able to make out more of the nightscape. Several hundred feet to her left, the paved walkway was a snake winding past the condos and disappearing into the dense shrubbery, as the blind white orbs of the lamp-post fixtures vibrated in the gale. Now one of the spherical bulbs tore loose and exploded on the stones. She was thankful that she had not taken the long way home.

Then all she could think about was getting there.

Would Lee be waiting?

Her stomach clenched as she realized that he might be trapped outside the grounds, unable to open the electric gates now that the power was off. He had his keys. But the front gate was still jammed. Was there another way? Yes, through the underground garage. He could walk in, if necessary, and climb the stairs. He might be at the house already, with a flashlight to show her the way.

"Jenny . . . ?"

Libby's voice, fading.

"The house!" Jenny called.

Her words blew back. Could Libby hear her?

She passed through a canyon of buildings, all dark. The windows might have been tiers of tarnished nameplates in the walls of a mausoleum. Were there really people inside? Her neighbors were nowhere to be seen. The only movement at the sides of her vision was of trees and the dense semitropical shrubbery shivering in the wind, the only sounds the wind catching in the shells of her ears. She refused to look too closely at the shifting shadows and moved on.

She ascended a grassy hillock and came down into an open glade. Her house was just over the next rise. She hurried toward it, ignoring the odd shapes on the ground under an acacia tree.

Straight ahead, there was a sudden flash as a telephone pole sparked on the street, illuminating the boundary wall. Now a shower of charged particles fell from the power line. A tree branch was caught in the wires. She wondered where it had come from; the trees on the street were topped and trimmed regularly by the city. Had one of the trees in her backyard split and fallen?

She must report the damage before a fire started.

She recognized the shape of her roof and the glinting windows were exactly where she expected them to be. She started to run, and fell as her rubber soles skidded in the grass. She kicked the shoes off and ran on in spongy socks.

She lunged for the front door. Thank God it was unlocked. Had she left it that way? Yes. The keys were in her purse, and her purse . . .

Inside, she was blind again.

Crossing the living room, she bumped into the table.

"Lee? Are you here?"

No.

She held her panic in check. The phone—she needed to call and report the power line.

And the body.

She could not get the image of Walter's ruined face out of her mind.

Were the police already on their way to question her about the other death, the one this afternoon? They would think she was a regular fount of knowledge about murders, the source of the Nile.

Just call 911, she thought, and tell them that the world is falling apart, that the madness is out of control and the chaos spreading without anyone to stop it.

Help. That was all she would say. *Send help before it's too late!*

She felt for the phone on the glass tabletop, where she had left it. She had, hadn't she? Then why wasn't it here now? She sprawled across the table, moving her hands and arms as if swimming, searching for it. The handset was not there.

Had she hung it up before she left?

The kitchen.

Now she detected a dim light flashing from the other end of the hallway, reflecting off the walls, and heard a sizzling, as if something were burning in a frying pan.

That would be the power line, so close to her backyard.

She went into the hall.

Lightning seemed to be flashing through the kitchen windows. She saw white phosphor in the air above the yard as the power line spewed sparks. The interior of the kitchen strobed, as if an electrical storm had erupted in the house.

She found the phone on the wall.

But the cradle was empty.

Now, from the hall, the sound of the front door slamming.

The wind?

She had not closed the door. Or had she?

She felt her way back.

A wind blew across the living room carpet and whirled around her ankles, freezing her toes. She strained to see past the couch, the fireplace, the stairs . . .

The front door was closed.

Then where was the cold air coming from?

She left the hall and started across the living room, as something moved by the stairs.

Someone was here.

Before she could move again the figure was coming at her.

"Jenny . . . ?"

Fingers cold as ice touched her face.

"Jenny, thank God! I thought I'd lost you!"

"I thought so, too," she said, momentarily relieved.

"Are you going to tell me?" asked Libby.

"Tell you what?"

"Who was that back there?"

"That was Walter," Jenny said with difficulty. Or what's left of him, she thought.

"Oh God . . ." Libby regained control. "All right. Now. We're here, we're safe. What do we do? Let me think. . . ."

We wait, Jenny thought. For Lee. Or the police.

Whoever gets here first. At least she was in her own house.

Why did that not make her feel any better?

"Do you have any candles?" asked Libby.

"I don't think so."

"How about a flashlight?"

"In the kitchen."

"Give me your hand," Libby said.

"I'll get it. . . ."

"No way. I'm going with you."

They slipped past the bathroom in the hall and the door to the guest bedroom, the one that Lee had promised to fix up for her mother's visits. The sparks outside had ceased; Jenny hoped that meant there was no longer a danger of fire.

She found the drawer in the counter and pulled it open. She handled screwdrivers, tape, junk of every size and shape. But no flashlight.

"It's supposed to be here!"

"Calm down," Libby told her. "Where's your phone?"

"By the sink. But the receiver's not there. I thought I put it back. I must be going crazy."

"Forget it. It wouldn't work, anyway."

"It has its own batteries. If we can find it . . ."

"We still can't use it to call out. If it's cordless, it needs external power, too."

Jenny started to cry.

"Listen to me." Libby squeezed her arms and forced her to remain standing. "We'll wait it out. You're not alone. Do you hear me? We'll sit down, and stay calm, and wait. We're okay. This isn't going to last forever."

Isn't it? Jenny thought. How do you know that? We're trapped. We'll never be able to leave. We'll have to barricade the doors, live off what's in the refrigerator. . . . We can't go anywhere. There's a killer out there. Walter's dead. And Tip. And Jerry and Adrienne. Who's next? Lee?

Is he still alive?

"It's my fault," she said.

Libby pushed her against the refrigerator and held her there. "You're full of it, you know that? You had nothing to do with any of this. Did you? *Did* you?"

"Yes! I must have. It's all connected. Everyone who's died, and now this—it's because of me!"

"That's irrational."

"No, it's not! I'm the common element, don't you see? Someone's trying to get to me, everyone I know, everything I touch. *I'm* the one they're after!"

"If someone wanted to hurt you, they would have done it by now. They wouldn't take the long way around."

"Then they're trying to teach me a lesson."

"Oh yeah? What lesson?"

"That I'm no good."

"Oh, Jesus, honey . . ." Libby hugged her. "Who the hell ever told you a thing like that?"

Jenny pulled away. "And now you. You're next! Get away from me, before it's too late!"

"I'm not going to listen to this crap."

"Fine! Don't!"

On the wall, not two feet away from her, the red light on the telephone's base unit began to flicker.

"Well, look at that," said Libby. "The power's back."

The lights outside and the lights in the house did not go on.

"No, it's not. It's just the phone. The batteries."

"Then the circuit in the receiver is open. . . ."

"It doesn't matter. We still can't call out."

"Well, it looks like somebody's trying to."

"No." That couldn't be. "I—I must have left it open. On."

Did I? she wondered. Was the red light on before, when we came into the kitchen? If it was, why didn't I notice?

Now a sound came out of the tiny speaker. A crackling, as the light continued to flicker. It was the two-way intercom, so that someone in another part of the house could communicate directly with the base unit. The batteries must have been about to run down, because a broken, rasping static hissed out of the plastic base, the white noise of electrical interference.

A cold breeze ran down the hallway, grabbing Jenny's ankles again.

"And you left the front door open."

"Me?" said Libby. "No, I didn't. At least I don't *think* I did."

"You must have. I'd better close it." And lock it, she thought. With the deadbolt. Just in case.

She went into the hall.

As she felt her way past the bathroom and guest room, the air became colder.

"Libby?"

"I'm right behind you."

Why did that not make her feel more secure?

In the living room, the front door appeared to be closed. Outside the windows the grounds were still black, but edged with silver in the faint light of the moon. There was no moonlight showing, however, in the rectangle of the door frame.

"It's so cold!" said Jenny.

"Do you want my coat?"

"No." Jenny shivered and moved away from her. She went to the door and threw the bolt.

"Turn on the heater, why don't you?"

"I can't. It's electric, too."

"Then let's start a fire. Here." Libby found the fireplace and the newspapers by the hearth. "Do you have a match?"

"I don't smoke."

"Neither do I. . . . Wait." Libby thrust her hand into her coat pocket and came up with a book of paper matches from Viva La Pasta. "Sometimes I pick them up anyway, for souvenirs."

She struck one. It flared white, then yellow, then orange, then sputtered out in the cold breeze, leaving a scent of sulfur. She struck another match, protecting the flame with her hands, and tossed it into the grate. A glowing spot appeared in the crumpled newspapers, then died.

"Close the window."

"The windows are closed," said Jenny.

"Then where is that breeze coming from?"

"I don't know."

Libby held a third match to the newspapers. This time the flame caught, fanned by a rush of cold air seeking the chimney. Libby turned her face up in the glow and looked over her shoulder. Her eyes focused past Jenny, at the stairway.

"Up there," she said. "Maybe you left the bedroom window open."

"I don't think so."

Jenny felt the current of arctic air flowing down the stairs and into the living room, hugging the floor and probing for her feet.

"We'd better check."

Jenny considered the stairway, the darkness there, and did not move.

"I'll go," Libby said and stood. She handed Jenny the matchbook. "You keep the homefires burning."

Jenny watched her start up to the landing, climbing the stairs without the slightest hesitation.

"Libby?"

"What?"

"Be careful."

"I always am."

Then Libby disappeared into the darkness.

Jenny compressed more newspapers and stuck them in the fireplace. As they burned, she sat close to warm her hands and feet. She felt the radiant heat of the flames like the sun on her face. Within the flames, pictures began to take shape, pure energy transmuted into ever-changing forms, shapes that evolved before her eyes into a Rorschach test of light and shadow.

She saw a face, another and another, or was it always the same one? Each flicker lasted less than a second, but one of the forms stuck in her mind: an ordinary face, thick-featured, neither plain nor pretty, a woman with her hair swept up behind her head, over the full neck, the lace collar . . .

She was able to identify it from the photographs and newspaper engravings she had seen so many times in the course of her research.

It was Lizzie Borden.

Immediately it changed into another face, not dissimilar but younger, finer-featured, more closed and elusive.

Emma Borden.

Lizzie's younger sister, born of the same parents and reared in the same house on Second Street. The sister who had conveniently gone out of town just before the murders. The police had never bothered to check her alibi, had not even interviewed the friend she said she was visiting.

If they had, they would have learned the truth:

That Emma returned that morning in 1892, long enough to do the deed and depart again at once for New Bedford. No one noticed the carriage parked down the block. She concealed the axe under her long wrap, which also covered her bloodstained dress. That was why Lizzie's clothing was unblemished, and why the murder weapon was never found.

This was what Jenny had discovered, and why she had written the script.

Had they planned it together, the two sisters? That was the last part of the secret that Lizzie took with her to the grave.

In any event Lizzie had covered for her, never breaking, not to the police or at the inquest or on the witness stand at the trial, and not ever during her remaining thirty-four years. Jenny preferred to believe that Lizzie had not been part of the initial plot, that Emma had acted on her own and that Liz had remained silent to the end out of loyalty to her sister.

Sisters, Jenny thought.

One who had nothing but love and forgiveness in her heart, and one who harbored dark thoughts and finally took it upon herself to carry them out. One who taught Sunday school and ate pears in the sunlight, and one who wore black and moved furtively, hiding her true nature until it was too late. One who served the light, and the other darkness.

Sisters.

Libby called herself a Sister, one of Rose's group. *We were trying to help you, that's all. . . .*

Jenny felt her face flush from the heat of the flames and drew back.

Could Libby do such things?

She had read Jenny's research, had followed the project with unusual interest since its inception. . . . Was it possible that she had been inspired by it?

200

Why?

How far would she go to help a friend, a new Sister, to take revenge against those who had wronged her?

It was a twisted thought, the most disturbing one yet. Surely Libby was not capable of such deeds, not even out of a misplaced sense of justice for someone she loved.

Though it was true that Libby had been with her at lunch, had heard that Tip was rejecting the miniseries, a conclusion that turned out to be premature. . . .

No, it was not possible. She knew Libby too well. They were like—

Sisters?

No, she thought again. Absolutely not.

But if not Libby . . .

Then who?

Perhaps it had only been a carjacker in the garage, as the media speculated. A vicious but unplanned attack, for no reason of any importance.

And Lee's parents? That had to be an accident, regardless of what he thought. Why on earth would anyone want to see them dead?

Unless it had something to do with jealousy. The desire to hurt Lee, even destroy him, because he was her husband and in the way.

She would not, could not believe it. Not even if Libby now thought of Jenny as one of her Sisters.

The word was plural, Jenny reminded herself.

Sisters.

There were others.

And the most powerful was the woman in black, Rose herself.

Of course Rose was blind.

Wasn't she?

How perfect!

No one would ever suspect a blind woman.

Until now.

Jenny stood slowly. Her legs had fallen asleep, or were they only numb from the cold? Her entire body was chilled, her head cloudy from the pills. They had finally kicked in, easing the pain of her headache but also relaxing her musculature, leaving her woozy. She wriggled her toes, waiting for the feeling to return.

But there was no time to wait.

She took a poker from the rack next to the fireplace and turned to the stairs.

A current of cold air still poured down from above. It no longer chilled her. It only made her numb, oblivious to any feeling of pain or fear.

Try to hurt me, she thought. Or anyone else near me.

Just try, Rose, if you're here!

She proceeded to the stairs in a daze, the flames at her back, the iron poker gripped tightly at her side.

Chapter 14

She saw darkness pouring out of the second-floor bedroom, sinking in a black wave. A hissing filled her ears.

"Libby?"

Only the hissing, carried down on the currents to enfold her.

The darkness flowed across the floor, stirred by a movement beyond the headboard of the bed.

The pale glow of the moon defined the elm tree outside the window. Contrasted against the blackness its branches seemed larger now, extending into the room itself. Then another fragment of glass cracked like an icicle and fell from the pane, and she knew that it was inside.

A long, misshapen tree limb had broken through the window and now reached toward her, beckoning her with its crooked finger to come closer. The bed sparkled with diamond-like shards as the wind blew in. The poker went cold in her hand.

"Libby, where are you?"

Was that a body on the bedclothes, or only the sheets driven into snowdrifts under the fall of splintered glass?

"In here . . ."

Her head jerked to the right, where the voice came from.

She turned to the bathroom, holding the poker in front of her.

She tapped the door. It was locked.

"Libby?"

"I'm taking a whiz, do you mind? I'll be out in a minute."

The remark snapped her back to reality. It was so like Libby, who was her friend. Just that. Friends don't hurt friends. And they see to it that no one else does, either.

"The window," said Jenny, "did you see? I need to cover it. . . ."

"Wait, I'll help you."

"That's all right. I'm going downstairs. Maybe there's a board or something."

She used the poker to tap her way to the

landing. Coming downstairs, she saw that the air was thick with smoke. The newspapers had burned to fragile embers.

The flue, she thought. That's why it's backing up.

She went to the fireplace.

The lever in the bricks was only slightly warm when she pulled it. The flue opened and the room began to clear. She picked up a sawdust log and dropped it into the grate, sending a flurry of red ashes up the chimney. The wrapping burned away and the compressed log caught fire at one end with a cool flame and smoldered.

She left the hearth, and continued on to the hall.

What could she use to repair the window? There might be a piece of plywood in the backyard; she was not sure. If there was it probably would not be wide enough. She could push the dresser over in front of the upstairs window, but that meant moving the bed. Even with Libby's help it would be backbreaking.

A sheet of plastic would work for now, even a blanket. She could tack it to the wall. She knew that Lee kept a hammer and nails in the drawer. . . .

On her way, she heard something fall.

The sound was very close by, but muffled.

That meant it came from either the downstairs bathroom or the guest bedroom.

She raised the poker and pushed the first door all the way back. Firelight flickered down the hall from the living room, now bright enough for her to see that the extra bedroom was empty.

She had to turn the knob on the second door.

The guest room was a jumble of cardboard boxes, containing books and papers she and Lee had never bothered to unpack. The single window in the back wall was covered by a roll-down shade, a rectangle slightly less dark than the rest of the room because of the moonlight outside. Framed against the shade were several stacked cartons with their flaps up.

Jenny spotted an opening between the cartons, forming a gap wide enough for someone to sit. One of the boxes must have toppled over.

Why?

She imagined rats at work in the shadows of the house, and shuddered. The wind moaned and leaves and twigs pelted the roof, but that was not enough to cause a box to fall, was it? Even now she thought she saw a red eye peering at her from the darkest corner.

Surely that was only her imagination.

I'll take care of it in the morning, she thought, and started to draw the door shut, when she heard a sound from the living room.

She looked to her right, as if down a long tunnel, a cave at the end of which a feeble camp-fire was all there was between her and the night. The fire was dwindling again.

Instead of going on to the kitchen, she returned to the living room.

She saw someone standing over the fire. Someone with large shoulders and a thick body.

It was only Libby in her heavy coat. Jenny recognized her short haircut, barely outlined against the wavering hearth. She was attempting to turn the log by hand before the flames went out.

Jenny came up behind her and touched her shoulder.

"Libby?"

The other woman started, her shoulders drawing up under Jenny's fingers, and pivoted. Her face was white.

"Jesus!"

"Sorry. . . ."

Libby's features were lost to the backlight. "Where were you?"

"I was just . . ."

"Forget it." Why was Libby whispering, her voice no louder than a hiss? "Come over here."

"What—?"

Libby snatched her wrist and dragged her into the shadows. "Listen," she said, "don't panic or anything, but—"

"*What?*"

"I think someone's here."

"Where?"

"In the house. Stay cool." But it was Libby's voice that now quavered. "There was a poker by the fireplace, remember? I saw it. Well, it's not there now."

"I know," Jenny said.

"You do?"

"It's right here." She held up the poker. "I took it with me. Just in case."

Libby started to laugh, tried to suppress it,

then threw her head back and let rip. The tension poured out of her until Jenny thought it would never stop.

"Oh, honey," Libby said, "I'm supposed to be the realist! I'm so sorry. . . ."

The laughter bubbled forth again and tears appeared in Libby's eyes. Jenny watched her shake with hilarity, saw her face transfigured as so much pent-up emotion was set free at last. She felt her own mouth widening into a smile, mimicking her friend, whose face was visible only as a line of small white teeth and two jewel-like tears where her eyes would be. Jenny giggled, then forced herself to turn away before the laughter became hysteria.

She stirred the fire, using the poker, releasing more red embers to spiral up the chimney. The log popped, giving off heat, but cold air still chilled her back.

She glanced around at the living room and hall behind her, and saw the walls licked by a reflection of the flames, as if her house and everything in it were about to catch fire and burn. At least I'll be warm, she thought, as one of the embers floated across the room between bands of smoke that hung motionless on the air.

Why, she wondered, would a spark move sideways, away from the updraft? It didn't make sense. It was dangerous, as well; the furniture or the drapes might truly catch fire when the ember settled.

Then she felt Libby's hands on her, rubbing her arms.

"You must be so cold," Libby said, no longer whispering. "Come here." She stepped in front of Jenny and drew her close. "Let me warm you."

"No, really, I'm—"

"Come on."

Well, it was only a hug, and for a moment it felt good. Libby was her friend. Like the sister she never had.

And, thinking that, she pulled away.

Something was not right.

Where had Libby gone this afternoon, after lunch? And tonight, when they left the house together and Libby went ahead to the front gate; where was she during those lost minutes?

At the rec room?

"Libby, where . . . ?"

She held Jenny at arm's length and looked at her straight-on in the firelight, with a direct, uncomplicated expression.

"Hm?"

"I mean, I . . ."

Jenny broke contact with her eyes. She was not sure what she wanted to say or how to say it, but she needed to know. She had to hear it from Libby's own lips.

"Where—?"

"What is it, Jen?"

"Nothing, I guess."

Now, out of the corner of her eye, she thought she saw the ember from the fireplace floating back this way, from the hall. Or could it be something else—the red eye of a rat, say?

She looked past Libby and saw that she was right. It was no ember. It was a red light, sharp and focused, and with it came a cloud of darkness, a shape that had no form as long as it kept moving, nearer and nearer to Libby's back.

"Libby, what *is* that? Who—?"

The other woman tilted her head with amusement and shrugged. Her lips moved uncertainly. "Jenny, I don't know what you—"

Suddenly Libby's eyes bulged and her head jerked forward, cut off in mid-sentence, as a thick wooden stick struck her across the back of the head. Her lips remained open, unable to find any more words. She did not even blink as a trail of blood ran down her forehead, collected at the end of her nose, and dripped onto the carpet in a starburst. Then she collapsed like a rag doll.

In her place was a tall, dark figure, taller by several inches than Jenny, with a short helmet of hair that glittered red, then yellow, then gray, then red again as the fire burned higher.

"Jennifer . . ."

Only one person had ever called her that.

As the light caught the face full-on, Jenny saw the big woman's mouth stretch into a vacant smile, her eyes giving off a strange light, a flame in each black pupil.

"Mother!"

The woman stood there, her walking stick in

one hand, the cordless telephone with its flickering LED in the other.

"Don't worry, darling. I'm here."

Jenny backed up, shaking her head violently as if that would cause her to wake up. But the woman really was there, and Libby's body was crumpled at Jenny's feet, lying across her shoes, holding her in place.

"Mother, *what have you done?*"

"Now there's no one between us."

"But—!"

"Don't thank me. It's only what any mother would do. . . ."

Jenny gaped at her. In the rapidly changing light she saw the big, rawboned woman, the broad shoulders and close-set eyes, the weathered face and the insanely fixed grin. She saw the long, anachronistic dress streaked with dirt, a hole torn under one arm, the heavy shoes, the peculiar angles of her posture, like one of the homeless, living in rags. The woman opened her arms.

"Now we can be together."

"You," said Jenny. "It was you."

"Come to me, darling. . . ."

Jenny raised the poker reflexively. "Don't come any closer."

"But, Jennifer, I only wanted to help you. . . ."

Jenny struggled to free her ankle from Libby's fallen body. "You killed Tip, didn't you?" she said, incredulous.

"Stupid man! He didn't deserve to live."

"And Walter?"

"That poor fool. It was his fault. . . . He cost us *money!*"

Her mother's singsong voice dropped to a harsh rasp. It was the other voice now.

Jenny realized that she had to follow every word, to limit her thoughts to the interior logic of the moment, however twisted it might be, in order to get through this crisis. Any distraction, any upsurge of emotion and she was lost. It was like a game, but one where her sanity and her very survival were at stake.

"Whose money?" she said. "It's not yours. It never was."

"Just you wait. When one door closes, another opens. . . . *Liz* will make us rich, you'll see! All the things your father never provided. A big enough house, so we can see each other every day . . . like sisters!"

"How long have you been here?" Jenny asked with perfect, blinding clarity.

"Not long. The hotel is adequate, but I'm ready for larger quarters. I think I'm going to like California. . . ."

That was why she had never answered when Jenny tried to call her. *She was already here.* Poised like a vulture, ready to swoop down and claim the bounty, as soon as the deal was set.

"You were here a week ago," said Jenny. "Weren't you?"

"So sunny! A perfect day for the mountains . . ."

Jerry and Adrienne never made it that far, Jenny thought.

"You killed them, too, didn't you? The brakes—was that how you did it, Mother?"

"White trash! They weren't family. They tried to marry into our money. . . ."

We're the white trash, thought Jenny. And you still are.

"That's right," she said, "*our* money. Lee's. And mine."

Jenny heard her own words resounding off the bricks of the fireplace, punctuated by clicks and pops and the creaking of the house in the wind. Her house, hers and Lee's. She thought her own voice sounded as unreal as her mother's, like the banal dialogue from a TV movie about a mother's attempts to reconcile with her estranged daughter and the daughter's stubborn rejection of her mother's love, because her mother was completely out of her head.

"Lee isn't in the picture anymore." And the woman smiled with satisfaction, as if proud of a secret that only she knew.

"What do you mean? He—he's coming home. Soon. Anytime now."

"Is he?"

A fear greater than any Jenny had ever known before swept through her chest and settled in the bones of her body. Her heart was beating so fast that she was afraid it would burst.

She grabbed the phone from her mother's hand.

"What are you doing, dear?"

"Calling the police."

"Go ahead," said her mother. "But it doesn't

work. I know—I tried to call out, to find you another agent. The line's dead."

"Where's my husband?"

"At peace."

Jenny threw the phone at her mother. The woman ducked and it missed, its red light tumbling into the shadows.

"Why don't you kill me, too? I'm no good, either! That's what you always said!"

"You had your father's curse, you poor, pathetic thing. You ran away, the same as he did. . . ."

Did he run away? thought Jenny. Or did he only try to, before you stopped him?

"But now you'll know what it means to be on your own," her mother said. "You'll come back to me."

Jenny was losing it, but she didn't care, not anymore.

"Don't bet on it," she said, and swung the poker at the hideous grin.

Her mother stepped easily to one side, avoiding the blow. Just as quickly she drew back her free hand and slapped Jenny across the mouth.

Jenny took the blow without flinching, and tasted blood.

"You bitch," she said.

The woman slapped her again.

"Go to hell," Jenny told her.

Her mother slapped her a third time.

"Don't you hurt her!"

It was Libby, on her knees now, clawing her way up the woman's body.

Jenny's mother brought the handle of the stick down hard, striking Libby with unbelievable force. Libby's eyes went wide with shock and rolled up. Blood coursed from her scalp.

Jenny saw the stick still swinging back and forth like a pendulum in her mother's hands, and realized what it really was. An inverted silver blade hung from the other end, half-hidden by the folds of the long dress. Before Libby could move again, the woman turned the handle around and swung it once more. This time the blade cleaved Libby's head into two halves, spattering her brains across the carpet.

Jenny backed off, unable to accept what she was seeing.

Time slowed.

She saw her mother turning this way, her mouth contorted by a hungry grin, her eyes blank as tunnels with nothing at the other end. She saw her mother moving toward her in slow motion, dragging the heavy axe, one arm reaching out for an embrace, the stains on her dress dark brown in the firelight. She heard her mother's voice break down into an animal growl.

"Come . . . to . . . Mother!"

She saw the poker in her own hand, positioned to ward off any blow. But the blow did not come. Instead her mother continued to rush her, fingers attempting to deflect the poker so that she could get closer. And as the fire popped Jenny saw herself thrust the poker forward with all her weight behind it and then her mother's chin striking iron, the smile distending crookedly, the lips flapping to shape more useless words before they ran with crimson. Jenny stepped back under the impact and one foot came down in the fireplace. She heard a sizzle as her sock melted, glanced down and saw the log breaking apart in a burst of fireworks, but felt nothing. She held herself upright with the poker and withdrew her foot, trailing hot ashes as she regained her balance. . . .

And in that moment she thought, I was wrong.

Wrong not only about her mother and what she was capable of, had always been capable of for so many years, all the way back to the time when her father had conveniently disappeared so that her mother could take absolute control of the household, but wrong about other things as well.

It wasn't Emma, Lizzie's sister, who gave Andrew Borden forty whacks. It was Abby, his hateful second wife and Lizzie's domineering stepmother, who had known he was about to change the will, leaving everything to his beloved daughters. It was Abby who sneaked back into the house instead of visiting an imaginary sick friend, in order to have it out with him one last time while Emma was gone and Lizzie and Bridget were outside. And when her pleas and her threats failed she turned finally to the hatchet by the back door and came at him in the dayroom with the rage of thwarted ambition. And

216

when Lizzie went in and saw him like that she understood what had happened and ran up to the witchmother's bedroom with the full measure of her hatred unleashed at last, and took up the blade and paid Abby back in kind, giving her everything she deserved, only that and nothing more. Bridget carried the hatchet and Lizzie's bloody clothes out of the house and said nothing because by then she herself was an accessory to murder. And the two sisters stood firm, one of whom was both guilty and innocent, one who had loved and yet turned to the darkness in a moment of righteousness that shone with its own black light, one who had killed and not killed, who lied and did not lie, who had done the only thing left in the face of the evil that she refused to call Mother. . . .

And as the last piece of the puzzle fell into place and Jenny's understanding became complete, time resumed its normal flow again and she saw only Libby, a pile at her feet, blood pumping out of the cleft in her skull.

She fell to her knees and pressed the sides of Libby's head with her hands, trying to hold it together, but there was too much to fit back in and the wound would not close.

She looked around the room.

"Where are you?" she cried.

She heard a whimpering.

Her mother had withdrawn, run away, shocked and injured. Now there was a rustling in the corner, a shadow on the wall, a flicker in the hall to the kitchen. The woman was able to move more swiftly than Jenny had imagined.

What about her hip? That was a lie to get sympathy. To avoid attending the wedding to which she so strenuously disapproved, because Lee was only a freelance television writer and not rich. And then to lure her daughter back home. But it had not worked. And it would not work now. None of her lies would ever work again.

"Come here!" Jenny shouted, expecting to see her grinning from the fireplace or hanging from the ceiling like a great black bat.

In the kitchen, the back door creaked open and closed.

"Then I'll come to you," Jenny said through gritted teeth, and went after her.

The backyard was bare. The other half of the elm tree had split and fallen over the wall but now the power lines were dark and quiet, the broken wires burned through and dangling from the branches like charred snakes. At the edge of the yard a bush breathed in the wind.

She grasped the poker in both hands and headed for it.

There was the whimpering again, but from the side of the house, and accompanied now by echoing footsteps.

Leaving the yard, she saw that the sidewalk was empty under an enormous moon. On the main path trees and shrubbery pulsed in the darkness. A shape blew along the path, too large and too swift to be a shadow.

"Wait for me, Mother!" she yelled. "I've got something for you!"

Jenny started for the path, then remembered the shortcut across the grounds. She bypassed the paved walkway and pressed deeper into the darkness.

Somewhere beyond the trees, a man was calling for his son to come home. Doors cracked open and people shuffled out of the buildings. Wobbling flashlight beams stroked the air and candles guttered in windows as if Halloween were already here.

It is, Jenny thought, and ran on, holding the poker like a sword.

Halfway across an open glade, she stumbled into a hole. There was a mass of spilled garbage at the bottom, leaking out of a ripped plastic bag. She got up and scraped her foot on the grass to remove its slime. Then the wind blew the smell into her nostrils and she retched. It was a dead dog that had gone stiff with rigor mortis, its forelegs frozen as if pawing the air. She prodded with the poker and its body slid deeper into the hole, leaving its head behind.

Nice work, Mother, she thought.

Then she wiped her mouth and moved on.

She crossed the next rise and came out by the pool. It swelled and ebbed like the tides of the sea under the moon's pull. All the chairs were in the water now, drifting under the surface like white jellyfish.

Beyond the pool were the rec room and the front gate. .

She'll go for the way out, Jenny thought. But there isn't any way out now.

She was not here yet.

Somewhere a siren screamed and somewhere closer a truck gunned its engine and roared around a corner. Somewhere people were climbing timidly up and down stairways as faces lit by candles appeared and disappeared behind windows in a ghostly procession from one room to the next. And somewhere heavy footsteps clacked on the stones of a path, grinding broken glass, drawing near.

Jenny set her back against the wrought-iron railing and waited.

Now a little boy came shambling across the grass toward the pool. He moved jerkily, unsure of his direction. He saw Jenny and broke into a run.

"Help!" he said. "Come quick! Please . . ."

"What's the matter?"

"Just come!"

Back at the top of the rise, there was another shape on the grass, only a few yards from the hole. He was hard to recognize at first, caked with dirt and mud.

She dropped the poker and tried to lift him in her arms.

"Lee! What happened? Where . . . ?"

"Home," he said into her ear, his words slurring and blowing away on the wind. "Going home, Jen . . ."

She held him tightly, caressing his hair, kissing his head. Some of his hair came away in her hand, along with a piece of his scalp. There was a long, deep gash under the flap. His collar and his shirt were warm and moist but his body was cold as ice.

"She killed him!" the little boy blubbered.

From the other side of the rise, Jenny heard the heavy footsteps on the path.

The footsteps stopped.

Now there was only silence.

"Go," she said to the boy. "Run, as fast as you can. . . ."

"Do we have to bury him?"

"Get out of here, before it's too late!"

The boy ran off.

Jenny had to get up in time. But she could not let go of him as he grew even colder in her arms.

"Leave him be, Jennifer," said a woman's voice. "He's not one of us."

"Neither am I," said Jenny, laying him down carefully in the grass.

Then she dove for the poker.

A heavy shoe came down on her hand.

"How can you hurt me like this, Jennifer? I tried to discipline you. . . ."

Jenny yanked at the ankle with her other hand. The woman toppled back, her head hitting the ground. Then Jenny was on her feet, raising the poker high.

"What are you doing? You can't lift a hand to your own mother!"

"Watch me," Jenny said, tightening her grip.

The poker missed the head and struck the shoulder instead. The woman grunted and scrambled for her weapon. Before Jenny could strike again, she was up.

"You're not my daughter!" the woman hissed. "I don't know *who* you are!"

The axe met the poker in midair. Jenny felt two of her fingers break.

"I don't know, either," she said.

At the sound of the clanging, faces disappeared from windows and candles went out. No one came to help.

Good, she thought. Now I can do this my way.

The axe came down again. Jenny kicked the woman in the stomach. The air went out of her for a moment, but then she rose again to her full height and finished her swing.

Jenny sidestepped, following the motion and wrestling the axe out of her hands.

When the woman saw what Jenny was holding, she ran away over the rise.

There was only one way out.

Jenny quickly outdistanced her, stopping at the pool enclosure and turning, ready.

The woman ran at her, hit the railing, doubled up as it almost cut her in half, and went over.

Jenny swung the axe after her, striking iron. Sparks flew. Then she jumped over the wrought iron and into the enclosure.

Then she turned, her back to the rail. The axe was too heavy to swing again. She held it sideways and aimed the blade at the woman's wattled throat, just below the chin, where the head was attached to the spinal column.

"They'll know it was you!" She was still grinning her impossible grin. "They'll see, and they'll know! You're insane! You're—"

"And you're dead," Jenny said.

Like all the others, she thought. Like my friend. Like my husband. Like you, you miserable cunt.

She set the sole of one foot against the railing, bent her legs and sprang forward, holding the blade in front of her.

The head came off at the shoulders.

A bell-shaped spray shot forth from the torso, drenching Jenny like hot rain.

Then the head sailed on in a high arc through the air. It came down on the water with a pink splash and floated for a few seconds as the pool became dark. Finally the hair caught on the upturned leg of one of the submerged chairs, drifting around it in a slow semicircle, like a boat at anchor, before sinking without a trace.

Chapter 15

In the morning light the complex was bright and attractive, the roofs of the houses and condominiums a striking addition to the skyline. The maintenance crew were nowhere to be seen, but they had done their job; the gate swung open easily whenever a police officer or paramedic wanted to enter or exit. There were five squad cars and two ambulances parked at this end of the street, pointed in the same direction. Despite this nothing seemed odd or out of place from the outside; it looked like the conclusion of a long night shoot on location, after the catering and equipment trucks have departed, with only the cops left to restore order and direct traffic.

It was too early for there to be much traffic yet, except for the Eyeball News van that cruised to the corner and parked in the red zone. On top of the van was a satellite dish. Two men climbed out of the van, drinking coffee and lugging cables and a tripod. They set up the tripod and mounted a Betacam on the fluid head, then patched the camera directly into the control panel in the back, as a man in an off-the-rack sport coat and striped tie adjusted his mike.

"Testing, testing," he said, and cleared his throat.

Another vehicle, an older Volvo sedan, drove slowly up the street and parked parallel to the police cars.

Two women got out, opened one of the rear passenger doors and helped a tall, massive woman out of the backseat. Then they led her to the gate and into the grounds.

Inside, residents gathered in loose-knit groups, speaking rapidly to the policemen, who took notes in small spiral tablets. A gardener stood next to a shining axe with a silver blade as he dragged the pool, removing the last of the chairs, while two ambulance attendants wheeled a sheeted body on a gurney away from the enclosure.

The rec room was full of detectives.

"The Friday Night Massacre," a crime photographer said to a fingerprint technician.

"The Axeman Cometh is more like it," said the print man, putting away his dusting tools. He closed his kit and stepped gingerly around the covered body on the floor, surrounded by mounds of reddish-brown towels. "How many does that make?"

"Three," the photographer told him.

"I thought it was more. What about the other male? What's his name, Marlow?"

"He's still alive. But I wouldn't take any bets."

"Four, then, if you count the dog."

They laughed.

"Who's that?" asked the print man, glancing outside as the three women entered through the gate.

"Amazon Women on the Moon," said the photographer, and they laughed again.

"The brunette is all right."

"Yeah," said the photographer, "real butch. Just your type."

"Like your mother," said the print man and carried his kit out, head down. He passed the three women at a brisk pace and let himself out of the complex.

The women hesitated at the end of the tunnel before going on.

"Are you sure, Rose?" said the small one, the brunette.

"Yes," said Rose, bobbing her head in a lazy figure-eight to catch the soundfield. "I saw it."

"We don't have to do this," said the stout woman on her other arm.

"I do, Marla," said Rose. "She's here. They both are."

They left the tunnel and walked farther into the grounds.

"And who are you ladies?" said a young policeman with a mustache and a long neck.

"We're—visiting someone," said Gail.

Rose and Marla kept walking.

"And who might that be?"

"I'm not sure of the address," Gail said.

"Hold up," said the policeman. "Where are you two going?"

"To sit down," said Marla. "She's blind."

"I'll give you a hand," he said, turning his attention back to Gail. "I'll need your names. . . ."

Rose and Marla did not sit. They continued on to the paved path.

"Wait here," said Marla. "I'm going to ask someone."

"No need," said Rose. "One is on the other side, I'm sure of it. She spoke to me last night."

"Not both?"

"Only one entered the darkness. The other turned away. She is with us now."

"Which one?"

"Her voice is weak. But she wants very much to serve as a Companion."

"I'm glad," said Marla. "Are you sure you don't want to sit? There's a bench. . . ."

"Isn't there another path?"

"There could be. I don't see it yet."

"I'm sure there is. Walk with me a bit more, do you mind?"

"I don't mind."

Rose left the paved walkway and passed through the trees and into the grass that was bright with dew. The ground was littered with palm fronds and acacia seeds; the cleanup truck had yet to arrive.

There were apartment buildings in this section, too, with groups of residents milling about outside. They lowered their voices and watched as the two women passed, the stout one directing the tall one by the elbow.

Rose stopped and faced the crowd, her white eyes aimed over their heads.

"Someone has a question," she called out.

No one answered. They turned away, suspicious, and drifted back to their apartments.

"You, there," said Rose. "The little one."

An apartment door opened on the second landing and a boy started down the stairs. His father restrained him. Then the mother came out and spoke sharply to the man and bent over the boy protectively, stroking his hair. Her eyes were as red as her son's, as if they had not slept all night.

"Don't worry," Rose shouted. "Pokey, is that the name? He's still your Companion! He always will be. . . ."

Then Rose moved away from the buildings and on across the grounds.

Near a footpath, they came to a circle of policemen.

"Here," said Rose.

"Are you sure?"

As they approached, one of the policemen leaned over, creating a temporary opening in the circle. A woman was now visible through the break. She was sitting on the grass, clutching a Hi-8 video camera.

"Jenny!" said Marla. "We were so worried!" To Rose she said, "Then Libby is the other one?"

Rose did not answer.

Jenny noticed the two women. There was no recognition in her eyes, which were so clear they were nearly transparent, like blue water on the air. Her hair was wet and disheveled and there was a fine spray of blood across her arms and face; in the sunlight it looked as if she had been painted with freckles.

The policeman leaning over her removed a pair of handcuffs from his belt.

"Place your hands behind your back," he ordered.

The Hi-8 tumbled into Jenny's lap, between her crossed legs.

"What about the camera?" she said. "It's my husband's. . . ."

"We'll take real good care of it." The policeman read off her rights and helped her roughly to her feet, which were filthy. It looked as though she had been standing in blood.

"What do you think you're doing?" said Marla.

"Stand aside, please," said another policeman.

"No, you wait," said Marla. "You should have a

policewoman present. It's the law. What are you trying to do?"

Jenny heard the question and looked up, a blissed-out expression suddenly animating the muscles of her face.

"I'm filming," she said. "We're in production, finally! And this time, I'm going to get it right!"

"Do you have a question, Jenny Marlow?" asked Rose.

Jenny considered but said nothing else.

"No?" Rose said. "Then I can tell you that you don't have to worry anymore. You have a Companion now, on the other side. A strong, older woman, who wants only to take care of you, for all eternity. I thought you should know."

Satisfied, Rose and Marla turned to leave.

As Jenny was led away her face went slack again, then froze in a blank stare, even emptier and more lost than before.